Me

Clara Andrews

For Simon and Ole.

A hangover lasts a day, but the memories will last a lifetime...

Chapter 1

Fighting against the clumps of mascara and false lashes, I try to peel back my heavy eyelids. How much did I drink last night? My head is thudding like a nightclub speaker.

The morning sun blares through the blinds, hitting me like a lightning bolt as I try to shake off the hangover from hell. Yanking the covers over my head to avoid being assaulted by the strong rays, I discover that I'm still in last night's outfit. The sequin dress, which I was convinced screamed sparkle and champagne, now whimpers cheap cava and is tainted with the faint odour of tequila.

A quick glance at my watch tells me I have just thirty minutes to get myself dressed and into work. I lay still for a moment, thinking of any excuse that I haven't already used to wangle the day off. Mumps? Gastroenteritis? Flu? Maybe an extreme allergic reaction would have a better response?

Without prior warning, I am snapped out of my daydream by the cruel screeching of my mobile phone. Snatching the handset from the floor, I frown when I realise this isn't my first caller of the day. My display happily flashes seven missed calls back at me. Unfortunately, they are all from the same number, the number that I least want to see.

I don't even need to speak to my manager, Marc, to know what he is calling for. After five years of working together, I can read him like a book. Tapping out a quick message to confirm that I'm not going to call in sick, I slip my phone under my pillow and groan. Being best friends with the boss does have its perks, but it also means that he knows me all too well.

Realising there's no getting out of it, I spin my legs over the edge of the bed and wince as I push myself up. My toes feel like they have been stamped on by an overweight elephant. That will teach me for cramming my feet into shoes that are a size too small. I catch a glimpse of my clutch bag and hang my head in shame. The ivory satin is now covered in beer splodges and what I can only assume are the remnants of a dodgy kebab.

Stumbling into the bathroom, I gasp in horror at my reflection. What stares back at me is somewhere between a homeless addict and Vegas drag act. I don't know whether to laugh or cry. Tearing my eyes away from my reflection, I strip down to my birthday suit and turn on the shower.

Stepping into the cubicle is bittersweet. As refreshing as it is to wash away the memories of the night before, the thought of having to get dressed and presentable for work is more than my throbbing head can handle.

After successfully scrubbing away all traces of congealed cosmetics, hairspray and fake tan, I wrap myself in my fluffy bath robe and stumble back to the bedroom. Plucking a black dress from the wardrobe, I grab my trusty pair of flats and turn my attention back to the mirror.

Breathing some life back into my hung-over shell is not going to be an easy task. Frantically grabbing my cosmetic case, I attempt to conceal the after effects of our *tequila team building session* with a mountain of makeup.

Fifteen minutes and a quick spritz of perfume later, I am ready to face the world. Armed with my designer handbag and favourite pair of aviator sunglasses, I grab my car keys and head for the door.

Today is going to be one of those days where even my coffee needs a coffee...

*　　*　　*

Jumping into the lift, I jab miserably at the shiny number seven and try to ignore the depressing nausea that is radiating throughout my body. Once the doors finally swing open, I make a beeline for the coffee machine. As I watch the murky liquid splash into the paper cup, I make a promise to myself that never again will an alcoholic beverage pass my lips. I mean, it can't be that hard. Loads of people are teetotal, aren't they? Maybe I'll even go vegan and do the whole bohemian thing.

Clutching my poor excuse for a coffee, I head over to my desk and drop my handbag onto the floor. The pounding in my head seems to be getting louder with each passing minute. Maybe this isn't a hangover after all. Maybe I am actually really ill and it's just a coincidence I drank ten tequila shots last night.

Collapsing into my seat, I scan my drawers for some painkillers. Quickly throwing back a couple of pills, I begrudgingly switch on my computer and load up my emails. When I am not feeling like a pair of Crocs I absolutely adore my job. From being a young girl, I longed for a position in the fashion industry, so landing the role at Suave was a dream come true.

Over the past five years, I have slowly worked my way up the ladder. As a newly-promoted Junior Designer, it's hard to believe that I started out making the coffees. Watching my sketches spring to life makes me feel alive in ways nothing has before. Shoes are my porn. They are my addiction. From wedges and stilettoes to cowboy boots and mules. I just can't get enough. Apart from flatforms. Flatforms should not be seen on anyone, *ever*. Go high or go home.

I look up from my computer to see a barrage of laughter falling through the office doors. Lianna Edwards. They one and only. I can't help but smile as she heads my way, clutching a couple of paper cups to her chest. Even after a heavy night on the cocktails, Lianna is still a ball of smiles and hyperactivity. I giggle to myself as I watch my lovely best friend make her way over to my desk, almost tripping over her own feet in the process. By her own admission, Lianna has always been a clumsy person. She blames it on being so ebullient, but I blame it on her skyscraper pins and canoe-like feet.

'Hey!' Lianna exclaims, flashing me a huge grin as she sits down on the edge of my desk. 'Here, take this.'

I accept the hot coffee gratefully and take a sip, allowing the heat to soothe my sore head.

'How are you so happy this morning? I feel like I've been hit by a bus…' I rub my throbbing temples as she tosses her blonde hair over her shoulder and laughs.

'I'm *always* happy!' She sings, jumping to her feet and grabbing her handbag. 'I'll see you at lunch...'

Nodding in response, I watch her work her way through the jungle of desks, totally oblivious to the many admiring glances she acquires on the way. I am about turn my attention back to my computer when I have a flashback to last night. My brow creases into a frown as I recall Lianna sashaying across the dancefloor. With a drink in her hand, she batted away the many eager suitors who were just desperate for her consideration. A fuzzy vision of dancing and laughter jumps into my mind, along with the alluring scent of men's aftershave.

Shaking all thoughts of last night's antics out of my head, I allow myself a quick stretch before pulling up my drafts of our new line. Something tells me that today is going to be a *very* long day...

Chapter 2

Considering my fragile state of mind, the morning flies by surprisingly quickly. Despite the growing desire to fall into a delayed tequila-induced coma, I manage to make it to lunch in one piece. Pushing myself up from my computer, I tug my beloved handbag onto my aching shoulder and slope off towards the toilets. Not in the mood for small talk, I avoid making eye contact with anyone as I pass by the rows of desks. The last thing I want is to be accosted by one of my colleagues, or worse, my manager.

Strangely enough, I haven't heard a thing from Marc since his many missed calls this morning. He knows very well how my hangovers are, so it wouldn't surprise me if he was keeping his distance. Over the years, Marc, Lianna and I have had many wild nights on the town. Each one resulting in the three of us crawling home in the early hours, with a chicken kebab and carry-out bottle of red for company. It has become something of a tradition that Marc will call me repeatedly the morning after until he is satisfied I'm back in the world of the living.

I knew from my first day here that Marc and I would get along. Just as I expected, it didn't take us long to discover we shared a love of Rioja, Dexter and all things Mexican. With his perfectly coiffed hair and retro glasses, he looks every inch the conservative, womanising gentleman he is ever so proud of being.

Slipping into the toilets, I dump my heavy bag onto the sink with a thud. As I run cold water over my wrists, I frown at my reflection in the mirror. My normally bouncy curls lie flat against my dry skin and the copious amounts of concealer I used this morning has done little in disguising the dark circles beneath my tired eyes. Hastily grabbing my makeup, I begin to attack myself with as much blusher, eyeliner and mascara as possible.

Once satisfied that I no longer look like the walking dead, I flip open my phone to a text from Lianna.

Bistro?
xxx

I slip my phone into my pocket and shake my head. I will never understand Lianna's ability to down ten tequila slammers and wake-up ready to climb Mount Everest. It can take me days to get over a bad hangover, sometimes weeks. Our alcohol tolerances aren't the only thing that separates us. Physically, we couldn't look more different. Lianna's slender silhouette and straight blonde hair make a stark difference to my dark curls and short frame.

It's fair to say that Lianna has been blessed with a perfect, statuesque body. It's a total mystery how she manages to eat like a rugby player and still have legs like a supermodel. I, on the other hand, only have to glance at a Big Mac for my cellulite to shudder. I often watch in amazement as she demolishes a pizza, whilst I miserably push a salad around my plate.

Leaning against the sink, I find myself wondering about the fairness of life when a couple of interns push their way into the toilets. Their giggles snap me back to reality and I jolt to attention.

Flashing them a smile, I take a deep breath and head for the door, reminding myself this day shall soon be over…

Chapter 3

The distinct odour of stale beer hits me the second I step into The Bistro, making me shudder with nausea. Cursing at Lianna's choice of venue, I squeeze past a large group of men, who are being unforgivably loud in the bar area. Trying to block out their ramblings, I scan the restaurant in search of Lianna.

When I am not hung-over, The Bistro is one of my favourite places to eat. Apart from the striking red menus on every table, absolutely everything is monochrome. The plush booths are always filled with happy customers and the distinct sound of glasses clinking together fills the air. It's retro, quirky and the venue of choice for city slickers on their lunch hour.

Finally spotting Li, huddled in a booth at the back of the room, I raise my hand in acknowledgement and make my way through the tables.

'Are you seriously drinking again?' I ask, giving her glass a suspicious glance.

'No...' She mumbles guilty, picking up the glass and placing it out of my reach. 'Are you feeling any better?'

I shake my head in response and search my handbag for more painkillers. The rowdy group at the bar are making so much noise and it's not helping my headache one iota. Throwing back the tablets, I look around the restaurant and marvel at how busy it is. Normally, it's just office workers and if we're really lucky, the cute guys from the call centre next door.

Picking up my menu, I try to find something that doesn't make my stomach churn with dread.

'Wasn't last night amazing?' Lianna grins and chews on the end of her straw.

'It's all a blur, to be honest.' I pour myself a glass of water from the jug on the table. 'All I remember is that we drank tequila and lots of it...'

'Did you see Marc with Gina from accounts? He tried to deny it this morning, but I've got the evidence right here...' She waves her phone around in the air and laughs loudly.

'What are you eating?' I ask, not wanting to talk about last night's antics for fear of throwing up. 'I'll just get some fries...'

'Is that all?' Raising her eyebrows, she takes the menu and taps it on the table. 'No starter?'

'Definitely no starter...' I rest my head in my hands and sip the water slowly.

As Lianna reels off our orders to the waiter, I lean back in my seat and yawn. The thought of crawling under my duvet is the only thing getting me through today.

Concentrating on my water, I listen as Li fills me in on her morning with the client from hell. The boisterous group at the bar are becoming increasingly rowdy and it's extremely distracting. Don't they have homes to go to? Places to go? People to see? There has to be at least thirty of them and I can't help noticing they aren't exactly teenagers. A little old to be acting like hormone-ruled boys at a school disco.

'Gastro Burger?' The pristine waitress is back and holding out a monster-sized plate of food.

Happily accepting it, Li claps her hands in joy and reaches straight for the fries. An oversized bowl of golden chips is placed down in front of me and I give it a dubious glance.

'Thank you…' I mumble to the waitress, flashing her a polite smile as she rushes off to another table.

Begrudgingly picking up a single chip, I nibble at the edge and try to force it down. Looking over at Lianna, who is merrily tucking into her ridiculous burger, I push my bowl to the side.

'Do you want some Pepto Bismol?' Lianna asks, reaching into her battered satchel and producing a tiny bottle of prominent pink liquid.

I take the medicine from Li and give it a good shake, momentarily mesmerised by the chalky concoction. Picking up a dessert spoon, I carefully pour the medicine and slip the spoon into my mouth. As I attempt to force the neon sludge down my throat, I begin to heave uncontrollably. Dropping the spoon onto the table, I cover my mouth with my hands and run straight towards the toilets. Pushing my way through the heavy door, I throw myself into a cubicle as the medicine makes a bid for freedom.

After flushing the toilet and tucking my hair behind my ears, I unlock the door and splash cold water on my face. Looking at my bedraggled, post-vomit state, I decide that I *have* to go home. Pulling a bobble from around my wrist, I twist my hair into something that resembles a bird's nest. I am no good to anyone like this. I'm going to have to use one of my holidays and call it a day.

Luckily, Marc's absence from work will make it easier for me to slip away. Drying my hands on a paper towel, I push open the door with my hip and walk straight into another person.

'Sorry!' I exclaim, letting out a nervous laugh and cursing myself for being so clumsy. 'I was in a world of my own…'

I look up into the face of my obstacle and I'm pleasantly surprised by what stares back at me. With chocolate curls and big blue eyes, his smile makes my cheeks instantly flush.

Quickly remembering I have just vomited and must look like death warmed up, I look down at my feet in embarrassment. Not seeming to notice, he flashes me a huge smile before continuing on his way.

As I watch him return to the lager louts at the bar, he looks over his shoulder and smiles again. My heart races and I try to hide my embarrassment behind a frown. Bowing my head, I shove my hands into my pockets and stride back to my table. Really not wanting another projectile vomiting incident, I try desperately to stop my stomach from fluttering.

'I'm really sorry, but I'm going to head home.' Noticing a blob of Pepto Bismol on my dress, I tug on my coat to hide it. 'I just need to get some sleep.'

'I was wondering how long you would last...' She teases, holding her arms out for a hug. 'I'll sort it with Marc. You get yourself home.'

'Thank you.' I manage a little smile as she winks and returns to her lunch. 'I'll text you later…'

As I make my way to the door, I glance over at the bar, secretly hoping to see him again before I leave. Scouring the sea of people, my heart skips a beat as I spot him. Confidently leaning against the counter, he sips his drink and laughs along with the others. Looking directly at me, he raises his hand and shoots me another megawatt smile. My cheeks flush violently and I practically throw myself onto the pavement.

Fighting the urge to look back, I head in the direction of the office car park, thankful that by tomorrow, today will just be one nauseating memory...

Chapter 4

I awake on Friday morning feeling completely rested and weirdly gleeful. Gone is the overpowering sickness, the throbbing headache and the mouth like a dusty sandal. Instead, I feel bright-eyed, bushy-tailed and ready to face the world.

Feeling rather pleased with myself, I pull my phone from under my pillow and scour through my emails. Noticing a message from Marc, I jab the icon and wait for it to spring open. My eyes skim over the message, taking in the gist as I go. Realising I have an impromptu meeting with our new designer, I glance at the clock and throw back the sheets.

Tapping out a quick response, I let out a lazy yawn. I'm quite excited to meet the designer as we're going to be working closely on the new line. This is my first big responsibility since getting my promotion, so I desperately want it to be a success. Thanking my lucky stars that it wasn't scheduled for yesterday, I allow myself one final stretch before hopping out of bed.

Slipping my feet into my slippers, I pull back the curtains and make for the bathroom. After brushing my teeth for the required two minutes, I hop into the shower wander back into the bedroom. Opening my wardrobe, I flick through the rails of black in search of my most professional outfit. I want something that screams confidence, elegance and creativity, or at least one of the three.

Settling on a navy trouser suit with a crisp white shirt, I finish the look with a pair of ankle boots. Twirling around in the mirror, I attach my watch to my wrist and quickly run a comb through my curls. Dressed to kill, I rifle through my cosmetic case and set to work on my face. Dancing along to the radio, I enjoy attacking my cheeks with various products and brushes. Beaming back at my reflection, I marvel at what a difference a good night's sleep can make.

Turning up the music, I dance around my bedroom as sunshine floods the room, telling myself that today is going to be a good day...

* * *

An hour later, I am sitting in the boardroom with a large Americano for company. A dossier of my many ideas for the new range is piled neatly in front of me and the presentation is waiting for our new designer. Satisfied that I am fully prepared, I pull out my compact mirror to check my makeup.

I am still touching up my lipstick when I hear the lift doors ping open. Shoving my mirror into my handbag, I kick it under the table and smooth down my hair. The boardroom doors swing open and in floats Rebecca, Marc's prized PA.

'Just to let you know, Marc is on his way with Oliver Morgan.' She gives me a shy smile and disappears in a cloud of perfume.

'Thanks, Rebecca.' I give her a nod and take a deep breath.

Quickly checking that everything is in place for the second time, I stand to attention as the lift doors ping again. Muffled men's voices drift along the lobby as the door swings open once more and in strides Marc. I can tell by the strained smile plastered across his face that something is wrong.

I shoot him a quizzical look, but he responds with a quick shake of the head and rolls his eyes. As Marc holds open the door, I tuck my hair behind my ears and attempt to smooth down my trousers, succeeding only in knocking my building pass out of my blouse pocket.

Cursing under my breath, I push back my chair and reach under the table in a desperate bid to locate the card.

'Oliver Morgan, this is our Junior Designer, Clara Andrews.'

Scrambling to my feet, I stretch my lips into my most professional smile. Only I am not smiling for long, as standing in the doorway is the man I spent all night thinking about...

Chapter 5

Okay. Don't panic. Just take a deep breath and...

'Clara?' Marc's voice is stern as he stares at me in bewilderment. '*Clara!*'

Realising that I'm staring open-mouthed, I somehow manage to regain the use of my tongue.

'Sorry...' I stammer, struggling to form a sentence. 'I'm very much looking forward to working with you.' Holding out my hand for a polite shake, I feel my cheeks burn like lava.

Less than twenty-four hours ago, this man saw me with vomit in my hair and Pepto Bismol down my dress. This cannot be happening. Marc excuses himself to grab some paperwork and I try to act nonchalant. He probably doesn't even recognise me. He probably has absolutely no idea that I am the girl he bumped into yesterday. Taking comfort in this idea, I feel my spirits rise.

Looking up from the floor, I offer him a tight smile and fidget with my watch. He doesn't look like a designer. The majority of designers we work with at Suave are greying, with enough Botox to smooth out a Shar-Pei. He drops his bag on the table and leans back in his seat, a smirk playing at the corners of his mouth.

Great. He *definitely* remembers me. I can see the amusement written all over his face. I stare back at him, taking in his chiselled jaw and piercing eyes. The fact that he's incredibly handsome makes this so much worse. I have a feeling I wouldn't be anywhere near as bothered if he was an elderly female with a walking stick.

Rearranging my stack of papers, I fight the urge to run away as his eyes burn into me. Why is he getting to me so much? He hasn't breathed a word, so why am I all hot and bothered? Racking my brains for something to say to fill the awkward silence, I breathe a sigh of relief as I am saved by Rebecca.

'Clara, could I just borrow you for a moment?' She smiles apologetically at Oliver as I follow her out into the lobby.

'There's a signature needed to complete Mr Morgan's working visa, so Marc has had to run over to HR. He has asked that you go ahead and show Oliver last year's lines for an idea of what we are going for.' She hands me a huge purple folder and scurries back to the lift.

Working visa? Where is he from? Maybe he doesn't speak English. Oh, please don't let him speak English! I slowly walk back into the boardroom and try to figure it out. German? French? Dutch? Are clogs back and I haven't heard? I take my place at the table and try to steady my breathing.

'Is there a problem, ma'am?'

He's *American!* My decade-long Matthew McConaughey obsession has given me the ability to recognise a Southern drawl when I hear one. Feeling a little light-headed, I'm suddenly grateful to be already sitting down.

'There's just a little HR issue that Marc needs to deal with, but he shouldn't be too long.' I open the folder and position it between us. 'He has asked that we go over the designs from last year to get a feel for the vibe here at Suave.' Flipping through the plastic wallets, I come to a stop at a page of studded ankle boots.

Oliver takes the folder with tanned hands and studies it for a second, before nodding and slamming it shut. 'Okay, I got it. Now what?'

'I'm sorry?' I stammer, taking the folder back.

'I said, *I got it.*' He repeats slowly, breaking into a grin.

'Do you have any questions at all?' I ask, completely thrown at his reaction.

'Where's a decent place to grab some brunch around here?' He runs his fingers through his hair and yawns easily.

I stare back at him, not having a clue what to say. How can he be so blasé about this? Who *is* he anyway? Suave may be relatively new to the fashion world, but it still carries a fair amount of prestige. Now I know why Marc seemed so stressed earlier, this guy is not going to be easy to work with.

'Excuse me a moment...' Grabbing my mobile, I push out my chair and stand up.

'You know, if you're gonna talk about me, you could at least do it to my face.'

Laughing nervously, I smile and shut the door to the boardroom behind me. I could kill Marc for leaving me alone with this idiot! Frantically bringing up his number, I perch on the window ledge as it starts to ring.

'It's me...' I babble into the handset. 'This guy is a nightmare! He took one look at the folder and said he wanted to go for brunch! How much longer are you going to be?' I pause for breath, twisting my hair around my fingers anxiously.

'I know and I'm sorry, but someone's royally messed up over here and I need to sort it out. Forget the portfolio and just take him out for brunch. Use your company credit card and we will sort it out with accounts later...'

'*What?*' I interject, panic rising in my throat. 'Can't someone else take him? What about Rebecca?'

'I haven't got time for your whining, Clara!' He growls angrily. 'Just take him out for brunch, tell him how fabulous it is to have him working here at Suave and keep him sweet...'

The line goes dead and I stare at the phone in disbelief. Has he really just hung up on me? Sliding the handset into my pocket, I tell myself to get it together. It's just a working brunch. I can do this. I mean, how hard can having brunch with a devastatingly handsome American designer be?

Chapter 6

After giving myself a quick pep talk in the lobby, we take the stairs to the ground floor and push our way outside. The two of us walk in silence for a few minutes, weaving between the hordes of shoppers until we arrive at the March Hare. With its low ceilings and original beams, it's a popular choice for those wanting to escape the hustle and bustle of the busy streets.

I head towards the back of the restaurant and take a seat at a beautiful antiqued table, stifling a giggle as Oliver ducks to avoid hitting his head on the beams. I'm guessing they don't have low ceilings across the pond. He flashes me that Hollywood smile and I feel my stomach flutter uncontrollably.

Once he is sat down, I push a menu towards him and shake off my cardigan. Whilst he studies the brunch options, I take the opportunity to give him a good once-over. His eyes are darker than I remember, but he is every inch as gorgeous. The dark curls that fall in front of his eyes are unruly and wild as he casually brushes them out of his face.

Looking up from his menu, he seems quite pleased to catch me staring at him. Blushing, I immediately look away and signal for the waitress. The petite girl bounds over and happily takes my order for a sparkling water and tuna sandwich. Turning her attention to Oliver, her cheeks turn pink as she scribbles down his request for a bacon cheeseburger and sweet potato fries. He might be in a traditional English pub, but the American in him is alive and kicking.

Smiling at the stereotypical choice, I decide that we have been sat in silence for far too long.

'So, how long have you been in London?' I ask, toying with the edge of the menu and silently wishing for a cocktail.

'I flew in Monday evening.' He replies, staring at me intently.

'Is this your first time here?'

'No, I actually spent a few years travelling in my twenties. I made some good friends here.' His eyes crinkle into a smile and I can't help but return it.

The waitress returns with our drinks and leaves a basket of bread rolls on the table. Not hesitating, Oliver immediately takes one and expertly pours the balsamic vinegar and oil into a pretty swirl on his side plate. He places it between us and I pause for a moment before ripping a crusty roll and dunking it into the dressing.

'Have you always worked in fashion?' I ask, with a mouthful of delicious bread.

'Back in America, I used to work as a photographer for Flash magazine. We had a blast. I loved being on the road, but when I hit thirty I decided I wanted something more settled.' He pauses for breath and wipes his fingers on a napkin. 'I applied for a Junior Designer job on a whim and it turned out I was pretty good at it. Four years later and here I am, head-hunted from six thousand miles away. Pretty sweet if you ask me.'

'Flash magazine?' I try not to show how impressed I am and offer a little smile instead.

He nods and returns to his bread, happily wiping up the last of the dressing. For a second, I wonder if I should mention yesterday's Bistro incident, but Oliver speaks up before I have the chance.

'Are you a local girl, Clara?'

I feel my stomach drop at the mention of my name.

'Pretty much. I was born and raised in Knutsford, which is up North, but my parents moved down here when I was just five.'

Oliver stares at me for a moment, before leaning back and chuckling to himself. Before I can ask what is so funny, our waitress returns and presents us with our meals. My stomach growls as I pick up my sandwich, suddenly remembering I skipped breakfast.

'Have you found a place to live yet?' I ask, reaching for my water. 'Marc mentioned that you might be here for a while.'

'Not yet.' He shakes his head and bites into the burger. 'I'm currently staying at The Wilshire. You know it?'

'Very nice…' I reply, rather impressed at his choice of hotel. 'You know, there's a house on my avenue that has just come up for rent.'

'Is Monday through Friday not enough for you? You want to see me outside the office, too?'

Blood rushes to my face and I desperately try to hide it. Biting the inside of my cheek, I will my face to return to its usual colour. Nibbling on my sandwich, I rack my brains for something to say to change the subject. Anything at all that can't possibly be taken the wrong way. The weather? The strength of the Euro? Madonna's greatest hits? No, Like a Virgin makes it way too risky.

'So, tell me, Clara… do you have a boyfriend?'

Oh, no…

Chapter 7

After embarrassingly admitting that I don't have a boyfriend, we eat the rest of our food in an uncomfortable silence. Well, uncomfortable on my behalf, anyway. Oliver seems blissfully happily tucking into his meaty burger, totally oblivious to the humongous elephant in the room.

Finishing my sandwich, I fight the urge to wrestle a spring onion out of my back molar and watch Oliver wipe his plate clean. Why do I let this man bother me so much? He might be very handsome, but at the end of the day, he is just a guy like any other. What is it about him that gets under my skin?

'All finished?' The waitress whips away our used plates with a flourish, quickly replacing them with a very tempting dessert menu. 'Can I get you any more drinks?'

'I'll have another sparkling water, thank you.' I reply with a smile, not bothering to look at the desserts.

Nodding in response, she turns to face to Oliver. 'Anything for you?'

'Actually, can I get a Guinness?'

She makes a quick squiggle in a tiny notepad and marches off with our plates piled high.

'A Guinness?' I ask, once she is out of earshot.

'When in Rome…' He gives me a wink and snatches the dessert menu off the table.

'You do know that Guinness is *Irish*, don't you?' I suppress a smile and dig to the bottom of my bag for my phone.

He shrugs casually and leans back in his seat, stretching his arms over his head like a teenager.

'I'm gonna take the chocolate brownie. If you're gonna do it wrong, do it right.' He flicks the laminated menu across the table and I immediately pass it back to him.

'Oh, come on! Don't be such a party pooper!'

I catch his eye and my lips automatically stretch into a smile as the waitress appears back at our table with our drinks.

'Have you guys decided?'

Oliver springs to life and sits up straight. 'Can we get the chocolate brownie, please? Two spoons.'

Before I can protest, the waitress speeds off with the menus tucked under her arm. Two spoons? Why has he asked for two spoons? Two spoons make it look like a date. This feels really weird and totally inappropriate. When Marc said to take him for brunch, I'm pretty sure he meant a quick sandwich and a lot of work talk. I can't even imagine going back and telling him we've shared a chocolate brownie and washed it down with a pint of Guinness.

I really need to speak to him and find out what's going on. Surely it is safe to head back now.

'I'm just going to nip outside and make a phone call.' Chucking my phone into my handbag, I leave Oliver to enjoy his Guinness and slip out into the beer garden.

I really hope he doesn't want another one. I can't take him back pissed, Marc would go mental. Perching on the nearest bench, I grab my phone and speed-dial Marc. It rings for what feels like an eternity before clicking through to his voicemail. Hanging up, I bite my lip in frustration. There's absolutely no way he is palming Oliver off on me all day.

Taking out my compact mirror, I reach for my lipstick when my phone starts to ring.

'Hi, Clara.' Rebecca's gentle voice floats down the line as soon as I pick up.

'How are things going over there?' I ask, crossing my fingers that everything is okay.

'A little better. Oliver's work permit has been submitted successfully…'

'Excellent.' I breathe a sigh of relief and tuck a stray strand of hair behind my ear. 'Should we head back over to the office?'

'That's actually why I'm calling. Marc has had to rush off to Ethereal. He has asked that you take a half-day and inform Oliver that we will postpone the introduction meeting until Monday morning.'

Half-day? I screw up my nose and frown. It's not very often that Marc throws the term *half-day* around.

'Okay...' I respond slowly. Half delighted at the prospect of an early finish, half concerned as to Marc's motive in letting us go.

'I have rescheduled the meeting for 10:30 Monday morning. You should receive an email confirming all the details.'

'That's great. Thanks, Rebecca.' I end the call and toss my phone into my handbag, before heading back into the restaurant.

As I approach our table, I spot a huge bowl of chocolaty goodness and two dessert spoons. Pretending not to notice, I drop into my seat and reach for my water.

'Good news, Marc has had some drama with a big order, so he has insisted that we take a half-day and reconvene Monday morning.'

'Excellent. You can join me in a Guinness then.' He smiles and passes me one of the spoons.

I hesitate for a second, before scooping up a giant mound of the luscious-looking cake. Chewing happily, I suddenly wonder if I am pushing the boundaries of a healthy working relationship. Should I really be getting butterflies whilst sharing a chocolate cake with a Guinness swigging co-worker?

I catch the eye of our waitress and signal for the bill, taking another few scoops of cake for good measure.

'Any plans for the weekend?' I ask casually, trying to avoid eye contact.

'Sleep.' He drops his spoon and laughs. 'Gotta save my energy for my hot date with *Melissa*.'

Hot date? Jealousy hits my stomach and I silently curse myself.

'Oh…' I try my best to plaster a smile onto my face, but it doesn't quite meet my eyes. What is wrong with me?

'Yeah, Melissa. The sixty-something realtor. She's helping me find a place.'

Realtor? Isn't that American for estate agent? In spite of myself, I feel a swell of relief. He laughs wickedly and snatches the bill that has magically appeared on our table.

'This one's on me, Clara.' Producing a leather wallet, he drops some notes on the table.

'Absolutely not! This is on Suave as a welcome to the company.' I try to sound forceful, but it just comes across as coy.

'I insist…' Oliver beams brightly and tugs on his coat. 'You will have to take me to dinner sometime and repay the favour.'

Blushing a ridiculous shade of purple, I decide not to argue.

'Thank you very much.' I flash him a thin smile and lean under the table for my handbag. 'It has been a pleasure. I look forward to working with you at Suave.'

After thanking the waitress, we leave the restaurant and walk back in the direction of Suave headquarters. As we approach the car park, I watch Oliver dig a set of keys out of his back pocket and unlock a top of the range Audi.

Opening the door, he throws his bag onto the passenger seat and turns to face me. 'Well, Clara Andrews, I shall see you Monday morning.'

Holding his gaze for a second too long, I nod and force myself to look away. 'Yes, you will, Oliver Morgan. Yes, you will...'

Chapter 8

Filling the bath dangerously high, I chuck in a couple of bath bombs and sit on the edge of the tub. After polishing off a ready meal, I decided to grab a glass of wine and lose myself in this month's Cosmopolitan. My eyes feel heavy as I watch the bubbles sparkle under the bright lights of the bathroom. Letting out a yawn, I let my towel fall and step into the water.

As I sink down into the bubbles, I feel every muscle in my body start to relax. I tip my head back and enjoy the hot water washing over me, enveloping my body in a delicious warmth. Reaching for my glass of wine, I take a sip and grab my face mask from the windowsill. Once happy that I've covered all the troublesome areas, I pick up my magazine and flip open the cover.

Just as I am losing myself in a list of the best fragrances, I am disturbed by the high-pitched pinging of my mobile. That will be Marc. I've hardly spoken to him since Wednesday and for us, that's a lifetime. Drying my hands on a towel, I reach down for my phone. Squinting at the screen, I frown when I realise it's a number I don't recognise.

> *Would you like to go for a drink*
> *sometime?*
> *George x*

I stare at my phone in confusion. I don't know a George. They must have been given the wrong number. Flicking on the radio, I drop my phone onto the floor and splash around to the music. My mind drifts back to Wednesday and I let out a giggle. I remember laughter, dancing, tequila and Lianna's dodgy kebab. Smiling to myself, I open the photo album on my phone. Flicking through the pictures, I repeatedly hit *delete*. Sweaty nightclub photos are never a good look.

I work my way through the rest of the album until I come to a fuzzy photo of me and Lianna at the bar. It would actually be a good picture if it wasn't so blurred. Visibly very drunk, we are leaning over the bar with our arms around the bartender. He looks strangely familiar. I squint at his name badge and can just about make it out. Gavin? Greg? George?

Deciding he looks more of a George, I make a grab for my shower gel and start to lather up. I am covered in suds when a thought suddenly hits me. Snatching my phone, I read the text again in disbelief as my heart races.

Would you like to go for a drink sometime?
George x

It can't be, can it? Surely I would remember giving out my phone number? My mind flits back to the tequila slammers, maybe not. I don't think I would even remember my own name after that many shots.

Turning up the radio, I slip my shoulders beneath the water, telling myself the name badge said Greg after all...

Chapter 9

After a night of tossing and turning, Saturday morning comes way too soon. Why it bothers me so much that a single twenty-seven-year-old would dare to leave her number with a potential suitor, I really do not know. I'm still feeling uneasy as I fry my bacon for lunch a couple of hours later. Buttering my toast, I tell myself to forget about it. I'm not going to text him back or anything, so why am I letting it bother me so much? I'll just ignore the message and pretend I never received it. Ignorance is bliss.

Taking my bacon sandwich, I prop myself up at the kitchen island and load up my laptop. I am dipping my crust into a mound of brown sauce when the landline rings. Licking the remnants of my sandwich from my fingers, I make a run for the phone.

'Hello?'

'It's me.'

'Hi, Marc!' I respond happily, instantly recognising his voice. 'What's up?'

'I don't suppose you fancy a takeout later?'

'Only if you bring the wine…'

'Whatever, Andrews. I'll be with you at seven.'

Smiling to myself, I end the call and click the handset back into its holster. Heading back into the kitchen, I dump my empty plate into the dishwasher before settling down on the couch to finish my coffee.

After an hour of soaps, I decide that I should probably do something productive with my day and push myself to my feet. Dragging the laundry basket down the stairs, I begin sorting piles of black and white garments. Once I have stuffed them into the washing machine, along with a big dollop of fabric softener, I carry the basket back to the bedroom and flop down on the bed.

Despite my efforts to stop it, the infamous text message pops into my mind and I feel a frisson of excitement. It's been so long since I had any interaction with a man who wasn't Marc. Maybe I should text him back and tell him I'm not interested. I pull my phone out of my pocket and bring up the text. My fingers rest on the keyboard and I find myself hesitating.

Deciding to leave it a while longer, I slip the phone under my pillow and snuggle into the duvet. Running my legs over the soft sheets, I allow my eyes to close. Maybe forty winks wouldn't be a bad idea. That's what weekends were made for, right?

* * *

Peeling my face off the pillow, I try to focus my sleepy eyes. The alarm clock on my bedside table flashes back at me and I let out a gasp. How have I slept for so long? Stretching my arms above my head, I let out a yawn and roll onto my back. Suddenly remembering that Marc will soon be here, I hop off the bed and change into my onesie.

After unloading the washing machine, I put a selection of nibbles on the coffee table and dig out some takeout menus. Feeling quite proud of my impromptu spread, I grab an olive from the bowl as there's a knock at the door. I glance at my watch and smile. Right on time. Marc is known for being a lot of things, but being late isn't one of them.

Adjusting my onesie, I run my fingers through my curls and pad down the lobby.

'Hello! How are you?' I exclaim, stepping to the left and motioning for him to come in.

'What's with the onesie?' He grumbles, his brow creased into a frown. 'I hope you haven't been in that thing all day.'

What is it with men not understanding the power of the onesie?

'Here, take these.' He hands over two bottles of Rioja and shakes off his jacket.

'Good day?' I ask, pouring him a glass of wine and dumping the rest in the fridge to cool.

'So-so...' He accepts the glass and takes a big gulp. 'You?'

'I haven't even left the house.' I curl up on the couch opposite him. 'I did the laundry and rewarded myself with an epic four-hour nap...'

'You sleep more than a sloth.' Throwing a cushion at me, he picks up the menus. 'What are we having? Chinese? Indian?'

'How about pizza? There's that new Italian on Water Lane...' I trail off at the look of repulsion on Marc's face. 'Indian then?'

'Indian.' He confirms, opening the menu and studying it carefully.

Leaving him to make his choice, I head into the kitchen in search of a notepad.

'How was it with Oliver yesterday?' Marc asks, pushing his glasses up the bridge of his nose. 'I hope he didn't give you too much trouble?'

'No trouble at all...' I reply, trying to hide my growing smile.

'Why are you smiling like that?' Marc asks, an annoyed tone to his voice.

'Smiling like what?' I laugh breezily and try to brush it off. 'Am I not allowed to smile?'

'Not like that you're not! Seriously, Clara. Don't even go there.' He scowls at me for a second too long before going back to his menu.

'Have you decided what you're having?' I ask, deciding to change the subject.

Nodding in response, he scribbles on the pad and passes it back to me. I love our local curry house, but the fact they know my name as soon as I say *hi* does make me question my takeout habit.

Order successfully placed, I head back into the living room and curl up on the couch.

'So... Gina.' I say mischievously, already knowing this is going to rile him up.

'What about her?' He responds, not looking me in the eye.

'I thought you two were an *item* after Wednesday night?' I raise my eyebrows and take a sip of wine.

'Do you really want to play this game?' Marc leans back in his seat, a playful smile on his lips. 'I seem to remember you being rather amorous with a certain barman...'

Barman? My mind flits back to the text on my phone and my cheeks flush violently.

Hiding my embarrassment behind my glass, I shrug my shoulders and look away. 'I have absolutely no idea what you're talking about...'

And I honestly don't. All I know is that I have a picture of a cute barman on my phone and an open-ended text message. I glance at my phone and bite my lip. What's the worst thing that can happen if I text him back? One quick message can't hurt, can it?

Chapter 10

After my takeout night with Marc, I spent most of Sunday recovering from yet another hangover. I did, however, manage to squeeze in a quick visit to the hairdresser and a much-needed manicure. With my confidence boosted from the beautifying and a lot of self-encouragement, I decided to compose a response to the mysterious George.

After typing and deleting for the majority of the day, I turned off my phone in frustration and headed up to bed, telling myself that I would return to it in the morning.

Well, now it *is* morning. With a sudden burst of adrenaline, I snatch my phone and tap at the keyboard.

Hi, George!
A drink sounds great.

How about Saturday?
X

Before I can back out, I hit *send* with trembling fingers. My heart races as I clutch my phone to my chest excitedly. That was actually really fun! What was I so scared about?

With a wave of exhilaration, I jump out of bed and assess my outfit choices. My eyes scan the rails of clothes in my wardrobe, finally landing on my favourite dress. Plucking the grey peplum dress off the hanger, I toss it on the bed and turn my attention to my shoe collection. Settling on a classic pair of stilettoes, I wiggle into the dress and twist my masses of curls into what I hope is a pretty, yet professional up-do.

I don't usually go to this much effort for work, but this morning I have an uncontrollable urge to look my best. Taking a seat at my dressing table, I give myself a smoky eye and add a touch of red to my cupid's bow. Maybe I am going a little overboard for a Monday, but since when was that a crime?

                    *   *   *

'You look very nice.' Lianna observes, giving me an accusing look as I enter the office.

'Thank you...' I twirl around and hand her a coffee.

Gladly accepting the paper cup, she takes off the lid and blows into the hot liquid.

'Why are you so dressed up?' She asks, brushing a piece of fluff off my dress.

Thankfully, her phone starts to ring and she ushers me away. 'This will be Kate from Ethereal. I'll call you later.'

Picking up my coffee, I head over to my desk and kick out the chair. It's only when I sit down that I notice a sticky note on my computer screen. Taking in the message, I can't help feeling incredibly disappointed. Apparently, there's no need for me to attend Oliver's introduction meeting as we already got acquainted on Friday. What a total waste of makeup. Not that it was solely for Oliver's benefit, obviously.

Loading up my computer, I respond to my emails before pulling out my sketch pad. Losing myself in my work comes so naturally to me. It allows me to slip into another world, one where it is just me and my ideas. I can spend hour upon hour lost in lace and leather and not even notice how much time has gone by.

I'm applying the finishing touches to a pair of ankle boots when I'm disturbed by the vibrating of my mobile phone. Reaching into my handbag, my skin prickles as I take in the name on the screen. With my heart beating fast, I open the message and scan the text.

Saturday works for me.
Ice bar at 8?
X

Ice bar? Where the hell is Ice bar? A quick Google search informs me that Ice bar is a small indie hangout in the centre of town. Why have I never heard of this place? Clicking through the online images,

I bite my lip as I take in the neglected building and bar area. Telling myself not to be so judgemental, I decide to just go with it.

Sounds good.
x

I hit *send* and throw my phone back into my handbag when a thought suddenly hits me. Did I text back too fast? Isn't there like a two-hour rule or something? Have I just made myself look like a desperate bunny boiler? Trying to stop myself hyperventilating, I get up and head to the water distiller.

Filling a plastic cup, I take a sip and lean against the photocopier, watching Marc talk animatedly on the phone. Looking my way, he motions for me to come to his office.

Letting myself in, I notice him check his mobile and smile like a schoolboy. I wonder which lucky lady is on his radar this week.

'How did Oliver's introduction meeting go?' I ask, taking a seat opposite him.

'Don't ask...' Marc rolls his eyes and puts his feet up on the marble desk. 'The delightful Mr Morgan has insisted on having his own studio. Apparently, shared studios are not something he feels he can work with.'

I try not to smile as I picture the two of them having the conversation.

'Head Office has been in touch and we have just eight weeks to get the new line over to production.'

'Eight weeks?' I gasp. 'That's going to be tight...'

'It is, which is why Oliver wants his own studio to work solidly on this for the next two months.' He pauses and exhales loudly. 'This is where you come into it. You and Oliver will temporarily move into the sixth-floor studio until the line is finalised.'

Just me and Oliver? In our own studio? For two months? My heart starts to pound and I try not to show it

'I don't want any funny business, Clara. This is a big opportunity for you. This is your chance to prove that you actually have some half-decent ideas rolling around in that head of yours.'

'You can count on me, Marc.' I clap my hands together excitedly and let out a little squeal. 'I won't let you down.'

Motioning for me to calm down, he flicks on his computer and presses a few keys. 'After you've taken your lunch, make the move downstairs.'

I flash him the thumbs up sign and jump to my feet.

'I meant what I said, Clara. No funny business.' Marc glares at me and turns his attention back to his computer.

Reaching for the door handle, I jump back when it springs open and in prowls Gina. Her flirtatious grin drops the second she lays eyes on me.

'Gina!' I exclaim, shooting Marc a devilish smile. 'What are you doing here?'

'I… I need to speak to Marc about an overdue invoice.' She stammers, her face turning a bright shade of pink.

Nodding in response, I slip out of the room and leave them alone, trying desperately not to laugh.

It's not that Gina isn't a nice woman, she really is. It's just that she isn't exactly what I would call Marc's *type*. Being at least ten years his senior, she disguises her age with copious amounts of makeup. Her voluptuous frame is dwarfed by her generous chest, making her look almost comical in the animal print dresses she is so fond of. The black hair and red pout complete the caricature style perfectly.

I hear them laugh and joke with one another as I return to my desk and chastise myself for being so critical. If Marc wants to enjoy extra-curricular activities with the office cougar, who am I to judge?

Chapter 11

Grabbing my handbag, I push out my chair when an email pops up on the computer screen. My eyes widen as I realise it is from Oliver.

Are you hungry? I ordered pizza...

Pizza? Who orders *pizza* to their workplace? I stifle a giggle and hit reply.

Have you seriously ordered pizza to the studio?

I wait for a few minutes until another message springs into my inbox.

*No, I have ordered pizza to **my** studio.*

Adrenaline rushes through my body as I lock my computer screen and hurriedly touch-up my makeup. What is it about this man that makes me feel like a teenager again? My stomach flutters at the mere mention of his name. It's been a long time since I have felt those lustful vibes and I'm beginning to enjoy it.

Satisfied with my makeup, I head for the lift and dive straight in, immediately tending to my hair in the mirror. Impressed that my up-do has stayed in place, I stride down the corridor to the studio. Pushing open the doors, my jaw drops as I take in the scene in front of me. Pizza boxes cover every surface, filling the room with the delicious smell of freshly baked bread.

'You made it.' I spin around at the sound of Oliver's Southern drawl and feel my lips stretch into a smile.

'Why did you order so many pizzas?' I gasp, running my hands over the boxes. 'Who else is coming?'

'Just you.' He smiles confidently and gestures to the pizza. 'I couldn't decide what I wanted, so I ordered everything they had.'

Propping myself up on one of the stools, I flip open a box and take the smallest slice.

'This is amazing!' Swooning at the taste, I nod appreciatively. 'Thank you.'

'I'm glad you approve.' He rolls up his sleeves and dips a crust into the mayo. 'It's nice to see a girl with an appetite.'

I narrow my eyes at him and put down the pizza. Did he just call me fat?

'So, what do you think of our new crib?' Oliver mumbles, motioning around the studio.

'It's great. I've always wanted to work down here...' I return to the pizza, taking care not to spill any down my dress.

'You don't think it's too soon to be moving in together?' He bites his lip and I feel my stomach flip.

Not wanting to encourage him, I choose to ignore him completely and concentrate on the pizza. I watch as he happily devours his food and smile to myself. Considering he is so cocky and arrogant, sometimes he has a real air of childlike innocence about him.

Deciding that I can't face another bite, I push away the box and wipe my mouth on a napkin. 'That was great, thank you. You saved me from a soggy sandwich.'

'You're very welcome, Miss Andrews. That will be two lunches I've stood you. Now, if you want to take me out for dinner as a thank you, you should know that I'm a very busy man.'

I make a spluttering sound and try to disguise it with a cough. For the want of something to do, I pile the boxes high and place them neatly on the counter.

'So, Marc tells me you already have some ideas drawn up?' Oliver's voice is suddenly serious as he wipes his hands on a napkin and beckons me to join him at the workbench.

'I do, I have been working on this for a few weeks.' I reach for my sketchpad and position it between us.

I am so proud of these designs. They have taken many hours of mental and physical work, but I honestly believe they are fantastic.

Oliver pulls the papers towards him and studies them thoughtfully. A look of deep concentration is etched onto his face as he studies each drawing. Taking a pencil from behind his ear, he gets to work on a pair of simple ankle boots and I try not to feel annoyed as he mutilates the original drawing with a series of strokes and shading techniques. Does he have any idea how long it has taken me to create the perfect take on the classic ankle boot?

Suddenly putting down his pencil, he spins the pad around for me to see. The patent upper has been swapped for a distressed leather and the pointed front replaced with a slight peep toe. Studs are scattered along the heel and spill out onto the sides of the shoe into a series of metal spikes.

'Fantastic! Marc will absolutely love these!' I watch in wonder as he picks up his pencil and starts to sketch.

Designers usually have years to complete assignments and still miss the deadline, but Oliver has transformed my original artwork into a couture masterpiece in just twenty minutes. I have never worked with anyone like him before. The design process usually takes hundreds of drawings and fabric samples to achieve the perfect finish, whereas he is hurling final ideas down on paper in one quick sketch.

He catches my eye and I realise that I've been staring for far longer than what is socially acceptable. Tearing my gaze away, I feel his eyes burning into the back of my head. I really need to kick this stupid crush if we're going to be working together for another eight weeks.

Reminding myself that inter-office relationships are against the rules, I take a deep breath and tell myself to pull it together. It's just a crush and crushes always fizzle out in the end...

Chapter 12

The next few days race by in a cloud of fast food, fun and I have to admit it, a little flirting. By the time Friday morning arrives, I cannot wait to get into work. My usual morning routine of a quick shower and change has evolved into an elaborate military procedure. I have been getting up an entire hour earlier than normal to ensure I am polished and preened to perfection.

Being so wrapped up in Oliver has almost made me forget about my date with George tomorrow night. It feels rather bizarre to have a date on the horizon whilst crushing like crazy on another man. I keep reminding myself that it isn't a crime to find someone attractive, and let's face it, who wouldn't find Mr Morgan attractive?

I arrive at the office and head straight for the seventh floor, clutching a tray of coffees tightly. I haven't really seen much of Lianna. Working from the studio and ordering in lunch means that we've missed out on our afternoon gossips. Marching over to her desk, I frown when I notice she isn't here yet. Placing a cappuccino in front of her computer, I draw a smiley face on a sticky note and attach it to her phone.

Moving on to Marc's office, I push open the door and let myself in. A handset is glued to his ear and by the sounds of things, he isn't having a very good morning. Raising his hand in acknowledgement, he takes the coffee and flashes me the universal *I'll call you* sign. Nodding in response, I give him a little wave and leave him to it.

Good deed done for the day, I take the stairs and head for the studio. Just as I am reaching for the door handle, I hear Oliver's Southern drawl behind me.

'Good morning, Miss Andrews!'

My lips stretch into a smile as he follows me inside. 'Good morning!'

Handing him a coffee, I laugh as he takes a sip and grimaces.

'Don't worry, I didn't forget...' I produce a handful of sugar sachets from my handbag and watch as he pours the contents of three packets into his coffee.

'Better?'

'Perfect. Thank you.' He nods gratefully and lifts his bag up onto the table. 'I actually have something for you, too…'

'You do?' I squeal, trying to hide my excitement as he produces a plastic wallet from his bag and hands me a sheet of paper.

My eyes take in the text and I feel my stomach flip. It's an invite to an exclusive fashion exhibition in Manchester.

'I was sent this last night. I thought it might be useful to go up there and try to get some inspiration. Check out the competition, that kind of thing.'

'It's pretty far away…' I muse, sliding the paper back to him. 'Manchester is about three hours north of here.'

'In that case, we should probably set off on Friday.' He mumbles, taking a sip of his coffee.

'We?' I stutter, my heart beating fast.

'Yeah. I just need to square it with Marc, but I can't see it being an issue. You cool with giving up your weekend for this? It will be educational, I promise.' He winks and throws the now empty paper cup in the bin.

'Are you kidding me? I'd love to go! Marc goes to these things all the time.'

'Then he shouldn't have a problem with us going. I'll go clear it with him.' Jumping down from his stool, he shoves the flyer into his pocket. 'Can you have a look through the fabric samples we received yesterday?'

'I'm on it.' I watch him leave the studio and cross my fingers that Marc goes for this.

Butterflies flutter in my stomach at the thought of a weekend away and I try to shake it off. Making a grab for the sample book, I open a text document on the laptop and start making notes.

A hot date tomorrow and a possible weekend away with Oliver. This could be about to get interesting...

* * *

As Oliver and I lock up the studio that evening, I am really looking forward to getting home. Rumour has it there's a hot bubble bath with my name written all over it. The chaos of today has left me well and truly exhausted. After Marc initially declined Oliver's request, I took it upon myself to plead our case further. I practically had to beg him to agree. I don't know what his problem is. It's not like anything is going to happen and it will most definitely prove useful in the design process. Besides, you would think he would be cool with office relationships being on the menu, considering he has been having Gina for dessert all week.

Walking towards the lift, I mentally plan my pre-date beautifying regime. I can't believe I am having drinks with a complete stranger tomorrow. All afternoon I have been struggling to work out if it is extremely romantic or just plain weird.

'Any plans for tonight?' Oliver asks, as though reading my mind.

'Not really. I might treat myself to a glass of wine and a bubble bath.' Stepping into the lift, I lean against the rail and stifle a yawn.

'Great.' He fires back, not missing a beat. 'Let me take you out for dinner.'

I feel every muscle in my body tighten and momentarily lose the ability to speak. I can't go out for dinner with him! It's against the rules! I look up at him and feel my knees go weak. Marc would go crazy. How do I say no? How do I turn down the hottest man I have ever met? Clearing my throat, I prepare myself to politely decline.

'Okay.' The word tumbles out of my mouth before I can stop it.

'Fantastic.' He beams back at me as the lift doors ping open. 'Come on, let's go...'

Chapter 13

Sipping wine opposite Oliver feels incredibly surreal and weirdly, very normal. My initial panic at having dinner with him intensified when we pulled up outside La Fleur, a quirky French restaurant famed for its champagne and lobster. Throughout the course of this evening, Oliver has spared no expense and I really do feel rather spoilt.

Upon arriving at the restaurant, he ordered for both of us and chose a rather pricey bottle of red. The amazing food and wine have relaxed me massively and I have to admit, I am really enjoying myself. I've finally stopped worrying about Marc and convinced myself that it's only a meal with a colleague. Just like when I go out with Lianna. The exception being that I don't fancy the pants off Lianna.

'So, how does a girl as pretty as you end up single?' Oliver asks, taking a deep slug of his wine.

I let out an embarrassed laugh and peek at him over the rim of my glass. His expression is unreadable as he stares back at me, his eyes fixed on mine. I feel my skin prickle and bite my lip to stop myself from burning up. Okay, this is *definitely* breaking the rules. What was I thinking? I really need to get this back onto a work-related path before it gets out of hand. I pause for a second, racking my brains for a platonic answer before speaking.

'I've always been truly dedicated to furthering my career. When you are completely committed to your occupation, it makes you very independent, leaving little time for anything or anyone else.' Feeling quite pleased with my diplomatic reply, I lean back in my seat and sip my wine.

'Nice script, but I didn't want the interview answer.' The flickering candle between us makes his eyes glint as he studies my face carefully.

Thankfully, I am saved by the return of our waiter. Placing our sizzling plates down on the table, he wishes us *bon appetite* before disappearing into the kitchen. Not being able to suppress my caveman instincts, I pick up my cutlery and dive in, glad to have an excuse not to talk for a while.

With the portions being so tiny, it doesn't take us long to clear our plates.

'Good?' Oliver asks, putting down his cutlery and pushing away his plate.

'Amazing.' I nod enthusiastically and drain my glass. 'I can't believe I haven't been here before.'

I catch a glimpse of my watch and realise it's almost midnight. I guess that's my pamper evening out of the window.

'How's your house hunting going?' I ask, leaning forward and resting my elbows on the table. 'Did you manage to find a place?'

Nodding in response, he fishes his phone out of his pocket and taps at the keypad. 'I signed on an apartment in Limechurch yesterday.'

He slides the handset across the table and I squint at the photo on the screen.

The website I am looking at is a Rightmove listing for a penthouse on the outskirts of town. It has four bedrooms, three bathrooms and is decorated throughout in opulent shades of cream and gold. I suddenly feel ridiculous for suggesting the modest semi on the corner of my street.

'Wow...' I breathe, scrolling through the images in amazement.

'You like it?' He takes the phone back and places it next to his glass. 'It's not exactly what I wanted, but it's available on a short-term lease and I can move in right away.'

'It's amazing!' I exclaim, unable to contain myself. 'I love it!'

'Glad you approve, Miss Andrews.' He lets out a low laugh and scratches his chin. 'Ideally, I would buy a property, but I don't want to commit myself without knowing how long I will be here.'

The realisation that Oliver will be returning to America gives me a wave of sadness. He's only been here for seven days, but it already feels like an eternity. The friendly waiter reappears and swaps our empty plates with two pots of Crème Brulee.

Returning my attention to my dessert, I crack the top with my spoon and marvel at how much fun I have had tonight. Oliver has been a true gentleman all evening. In any other circumstances, this would be the perfect date. My feelings towards him have grown over the course of this week and after tonight, I am confident that those feelings are reciprocated.

I have to put a stop to this. It's not professional and as I keep reminding myself, it's against the bloody rules. I value my job way too much to throw it away by getting involved with a colleague, especially a colleague that will be jetting back to America in the not so distant future. From now on, my relationship with Oliver will be purely platonic.

'Ready to go?' Oliver asks, signalling for the bill.

'I am, thank you for a fabulous evening.' I raise my now empty glass and clink it against his. 'I've had a lovely time.'

'You are very welcome. We will have to do it again sometime.

I smile back at him, my head yelling *no*, but my heart screaming *yes*.

'Most definitely...'

Chapter 14

I lay in bed on Saturday morning reminiscing over my meal with Oliver. It's been a long time since I have been wined and dined. Oliver is totally different to the men I have dated in the past. He's so confident and knows exactly what he wants. It's so refreshing to meet a real man as opposed to the silly boys I am normally attracted to.

Reminding myself that I have a date tonight, I allow myself a final stretch before throwing back the covers. It feels quite bizarre to have a post-date high coupled with pre-date nerves. I have no idea what to expect from George. I don't know anything about him, but I do know he will have to pull it out of the bag if he wants to beat last night. Oliver has set the bar astronomically high with champagne and lobster at La Fleur.

Remembering that we're meeting at a student hangout, I try not to get my hopes up. I haven't been to a place like Ice bar since I was twenty-one and going through my Arctic Monkeys phase. What does one wear to an indie club these days? Padding over to my wardrobe, I pull out some skinny jeans and hang them on the door handle. You can't really go wrong with skinny jeans, can you? I study the rail for a while longer, before plucking a low-cut red blouse from the rack. Simple, sophisticated and not too librarian.

Satisfied with my outfit, I flick on the radio and pour my nail polish collection onto the bed. Immediately picking out a deep scarlet and glossy top-coat, I sing along to the music and head into the bathroom. Despite my efforts to keep Oliver off my mind, I can't help but wonder what he is doing tonight. Maybe he's on a date, too. The thought of it makes my stomach churn with envy. If I am lusting over Oliver, why on earth am I going on a date with a guy I don't even remember meeting?

Perching on the edge of the bath, I try and fail to find a reason for going through with my date with George, but with Oliver off the menu, I can't find a reason not to...

*   *   *

The taxi swings into the fast lane and I try to ignore the growing sickness in my stomach. I have spent no less than three hours getting ready for tonight and I have to admit that I'm pretty pleased with the outcome. My hair is glossy and tousled and my skin is golden brown. After a few terrible attempts, I finally succeeded in contouring my face and the false lashes I ordered online have finished the look perfectly.

The cab comes to an abrupt stop and I tell myself not to panic as I glance at the building. It's not that the place doesn't look nice, that's not the problem at all. It's the gathering of young girls outside wearing

Converse and hoodies that are causing me concern. I look down at my skyscraper stilettos dubiously and consider going back home to change.

Convincing myself it will be okay, I pay the driver and step out onto the busy street. As my mother always said, it's better to be over dressed than under dressed. Never apologise for making the effort.

Squeezing between the crowds of teenagers, I head inside and have to admit that I'm pleasantly surprised. If I forget the clothing issue, it isn't all that bad. It's bigger than I thought, with individual booths surrounding a small stage. The lighting is low and there's a buzz of excitement in the air as people talk animatedly amongst one another.

Thankful for the dim lighting, I head for the bar and have a quick read through the menu. Pointing at the first cocktail on the list, I leave the barman to work his magic and scan the room for George. Convincing myself I'm early, I pick up my glass and take a seat at the back of the room, deliberately choosing a table next to the fire exit in case I need to make a quick escape.

Sipping my drink slowly, I look up as a pint of beer appears on my table. My jaw drops open as a rather scary looking bloke with facial piercings and tattoos looks me up and down.

'Can I get you a drink?' He asks, draping an arm around the back of my seat and licking his lips.

'Thank you, but I'm waiting for my boyfriend.' I smile apologetically as he grumbles and reluctantly slopes off to the dancefloor.

Shuddering, I decide that George isn't going to show and push myself to my feet. What was I even thinking coming here? Clutching my bag, I am about to head for the door when I notice a man laughing at the bar. Raising his hand, he waves and beckons me to come over to him.

Is this him? Has he been standing there laughing at me the whole time? Feeling my blood boil with humiliation, my brow creases into a frown.

'You made it.' Offering me a cheeky smile, he brushes his dark hair out of his face.

'You're late.' I scowl before I can stop myself.

'Actually, I arrived five minutes early, but I overheard you saying you were waiting for your boyfriend and I didn't fancy getting a black eye so...' He rolls his eyes dramatically and I try my hardest not to laugh.

'Hilarious.' I mumble, tucking my hair behind my ears.

'It really was! You should have seen your face when he sat down!' Letting out a loud laugh, he composes himself when I don't return his enthusiasm. 'Drink?' He asks, pointing towards the bar.

'Definitely.'

Something tells me I'm going to need a lot more than one...

Chapter 15

Several cocktails and a few hours later, the place is packed out. There's a cool band playing music to the crowds of happy people and there isn't a spare seat in the house. I didn't have high hopes for tonight, but I haven't laughed this much in ages.

George isn't the type of man I would normally go for, but with his olive skin, chocolate eyes and tight curls, he's absolutely gorgeous. Good looking, cheeky and downright charming. As I listen to him talk, I wonder why I don't have the same tingly feeling I get when I look at Oliver. Those fluttering butterflies that hit the moment he walks into a room just aren't there.

Excusing myself to use the bathroom, I push my way through the crowds of people and squeeze into a tiny cubicle. After peeing and flushing, I rinse my hands before refreshing my makeup. The melted mascara rings beneath my eyes are usually a sign it's time to call it a night, but I look more part of the crowd now than when I first arrived.

Making my way back to our table, I pause at the bar and grab a couple more drinks. As much as I love cocktails, I think I should make this my last. Any more and I shall be seeing bubbles, not just drinking them.

Juggling the glasses, I drop back into my seat and pass one to George.

'Finally! I thought you had fallen in.' He winks and takes a sip of his cocktail, nodding in approval. 'How do you like the band?' Turning around in his seat, he claps his hands together as the song comes to an end.

'They're great!' I gush enthusiastically, joining in with the applause. 'I've had such a good time tonight!'

'Really?' He raises his eyebrows sceptically. 'I was a little concerned when I saw the outfit that this wouldn't be your kind of place...'

'What's wrong with my outfit?' I demand, motioning to my jeans and heels.

'Nothing! I just wouldn't have put you in Ice bar, that's all.' George places a hand on my knee and smiles. 'You look fantastic.'

Our eyes meet and I feel a frisson of excitement. Dating is so much fun. Why have I shut myself off from men for so long?

Chewing on the end of my straw, I listen intently as George fills me in on the latest indie bands. After a while, the conversation runs dry and talk changes to work.

'Suave?' George repeats, drumming his fingers on the table. 'That rings a bell. I think I have a pair of those.'

'Considering we only sell women's shoes, I find that really interesting…' I let out a giggle and toss my hair over my shoulder.

His cheeks flush and he makes a stab at changing the subject. 'Do you enjoy your work?'

My mind automatically flits to Oliver and our lovely meal last night. I picture his face and my lips spring into a smile. Feeling my stomach flip, I try to push it to the back of my mind.

'I do. I love designing and I love shoes, so it's a win-win.'

'What girl doesn't love shoes?' George laughs and drains his glass in one gulp.

Feeling rather drunk, I wave my arms around to the music. 'Give a girl the right shoes and she can conquer the world.'

'And what shoes do you have on?' He glances under the table at my stilettoes.

'Dancing shoes!' Jumping to my feet, I hold out my hand for his.

George shakes his head and points to his empty glass. 'I'm going to need at least one more before I get up there.'

Standing up, he leads the way to the bar and orders two tequila slammers. I watch the barman pour the gold liquid and ignore the voice in my mind that warns me this is a bad idea. Standing in front of George to avoid being squashed by the crowds, I breathe in his musky aftershave.

I hold up my tiny glass and clink it against his. 'To dancing!'

His eyes crinkle into a smile as he throws back the shot. 'So, do you normally give your phone number to random barmen after a few too many tequilas?'

'How do you know I had a few too many?' I fire back, reaching for the lemon and grimacing.

'Because I was the one serving them!'

We erupt into laughter and make our way over to the dancefloor.

'No, but I am glad I did.'

And I really, *really* am...

Chapter 16

Sitting in McDonald's on Sunday morning, I sip my coffee tepidly and listen to Lianna ramble.

'So, you went out with Oliver on Friday and George on Saturday?' She exclaims, her eyes glittering. 'Two men in two days!'

'I know it sounds bad, but I didn't exactly *go out* with Oliver. It wasn't a date or anything, just dinner after work with a colleague.'

'Right, because I always have lobster at La Fleur with the HR guys...' She rolls her eyes and laughs. 'Isn't dating someone you work with awkward?'

'It *wasn't* a date!' I break off a piece of hash brown and warm my hands on my coffee. 'Jeez, you're like a dog with a bone.'

'What was George like?' Li asks, twirling a strand of blonde hair around her fingers.

I smile and consider my reply carefully. 'Funny, confident, cute. I really liked him…'

She studies my face for a second, before letting out a gasp. 'You slept with him!'

Unable to talk with a mouthful of food, I respond with a violent shake of the head. Hurriedly swallowing and burning my throat in the process, I raise my hands in protest.

'I did not!' I give her the sincerest look I can muster and hope she takes the bait.

'Yeah, right.' She laughs wickedly, not convinced in the slightest. 'Spill the beans…'

I stare at her in disbelief. How can she always tell when I am hiding something? Am I that bad an actress?

'Okay. I *did* spend the night with him, but nothing happened. I swear.'

'I don't believe you.' She retorts, screwing up her sandwich wrapper and throwing it in the bin.

'Honestly! We met in Greenton. One drink became six and six drinks led to tequilas. Before I knew it, it was 2am and the taxi queue was a mile long.'

She crosses her legs and frowns. 'That still doesn't explain why you stayed over.'

'Come on, you know how far away Greenton is! George had a spare room. It made more sense to crash there than fight for a taxi back.'

'If you say so…' Lianna winks and picks up her handbag. 'I'm only joking. I believe you.'

Shaking my head in annoyance, I grab my coffee and follow her into the car park.

'Fancy a trip into town?' She asks, beeping open the car. 'It's been ages since we hit the shops.'

'Go on then.' I grumble groggily, slipping on my sunglasses.

Knowing that Lianna would rather chop off her eyelashes than let me take a coffee into her sparkling BMW, I toss my cup into the bin and brace myself for her wacky driving.

The last thing I feel like doing is traipsing around the shops, but a little retail therapy never hurt anyone, did it?

* * *

Collapsing onto my bed later that evening, I pour the contents of my shopping onto the duvet and run my fingers over the fabrics. Picking up my favourite purchase of the day, I rip off the tags and hang the turquoise jacket in my wardrobe. Digging the receipt out of my purse, I tear it up and drop it into the bin. I've always hated receipts. They remind me of little death certificates for the money you no longer have. Like, this is how that tenner died, keep it safe and mourn it forever.

Wandering into the kitchen, I head straight for the medicine cabinet and pop a couple of headache pills. Tequila hangover plus Lianna's horrific driving makes for one monster migraine. Rubbing my sore temples, I pad back into my bedroom and stretch out on the sheets. After my late night on Friday with Oliver and last night's epic antics with George, my battery is in desperate need of a recharge.

Once I have swapped my jeans for a pair of pyjamas, I crawl beneath the duvet and flick off the light. My eyes become heavy as I wrap my arms around the pillow and breathe deeply.

I'm drifting into a delicious sleep when I am jolted back to reality by my mobile phone pinging loudly. Letting out a groan, I grab the handset from the bedside table and try to adjust my eyes to the bright screen.

I had a great time with you last night. Let's do it again, but maybe with coffee and not tequila.
George
x

My fingers turn to butter and I drop my phone on the floor with a clatter. Crawling back into bed, I feel my lips stretch into a smile. Was that the butterflies I have with Oliver or is it the tequila causing my stomach to churn? Either way, I don't think I can stay awake long enough to find out…

Chapter 17

I am happily making my way through a steak baguette when Rebecca appears at the studio doors. Prising myself away from my lunch, I wipe my hands on a napkin and beckon her to come in.

'Hi...' She fidgets with her blouse and looks around the room awkwardly.

I follow her gaze and try to work out why she is acting so coy. 'Are you alright, Rebecca?'

Nodding in response, she continues to look behind me inquisitively. 'Marc asked me to drop these in for you.'

Taking the envelope, my heart skips a beat as I pull two train tickets to Manchester. Trying to act nonchalant, I pop them back into the envelope and drop it onto my pile of papers.

'That's great! Thanks, Rebecca.' I smile and wait for her to leave, only she seems frozen to the spot.

Suddenly springing to life, she flicks her hair over her shoulder and giggles. 'Hi, Oliver!'

I spin around to see Oliver pushing his way through the door, his arms laden with fabric samples and brochures. Offering her a tight smile in response, he nods and jumps onto a stool. Relieved that her crush doesn't seem to be reciprocated, I turn my attention back to Rebecca.

'Was there anything else?' I smile through gritted teeth and lean on the door handle, hoping that she takes the hint.

'No, nothing else.' She smiles shamelessly at Oliver before backing out of the room and scurrying off down the hall.

Seemingly totally oblivious to Rebecca's advances, Oliver loads up his laptop and pulls my sandwich towards him. 'You finished with this?'

Laughing at his boldness, I snatch the baguette back and take a huge bite.

'Didn't your parents teach you to share?' He exclaims, chasing me around the table and wrestling it from my grip.

Giggling as he tickles me for the sandwich, I hold it above my head as my sides ache with laughter. We lock eyes for a moment, his face just inches from mine. Tearing my gaze away, I brush myself down and hand him the baguette.

'Anyway…' Clearing my throat, I sit back and push the envelope across the table. 'Rebecca brought these down…' I watch as he studies the accommodation voucher and train tickets.

'I don't think so.' He shakes his head and bites into the sandwich. 'We're not travelling three hours for some cheap motel. Leave it with me.'

Cheap motel? I take the voucher and read over the residency details. A quick Google search brings up a basic website and a few dodgy photographs. It's not *too* bad. It isn't the Ritz, but I have stayed in far worse over the years. I contemplate defending the hotel, but stop myself just in time. A part of me wants to see what he can come up with.

'Good weekend?' Oliver asks, popping my thought bubble.

'Yes…' My cheeks flush and I feel weirdly guilty. 'How about you?'

'Yeah, great.' He smiles and loads up his emails on his laptop. 'Moved into my new place, did a little shopping, went on a date...'

'Date?' My voice is strangely high-pitched and I try to disguise it with a cough.

Date? He went on a date? Who with? I try to remind myself that I also went on a date, so why do I feel so bothered?

'Yeah, I met a real nice English girl. We had a blast...'

'Lovely.' I respond, trying not to sound bitter.

He leans back in his seat and folds his arms behind his head, clearly enjoying seeing me squirm. 'Took her to this little French place. Lobster, fine wine…'

I pause with my hand on the keyboard. Wait a minute. Is he talking about me?

'What do you say, Clara? Do you think that warrants a second date?'

He *is* talking about me! It wasn't a date! He never said that it was a date. Choosing to ignore him, I pick up the fabric samples and flip through the pages.

'What do you think of this lace?' I push the book towards him and turn back to my computer.

Taking the sample book from me, he runs his fingers over the fabric. 'I like it. Call the company and see what they can do on it.'

Picking up the book, I open my emails and begin to type out a message. As my fingers hit the keys, I peek at Oliver from behind my screen and mentally compare the two men in my life. George is so lovely, funny and kind. You would be proud to take him home to meet your parents. Oliver, on the other hand, is enigmatic, intriguing and enjoys keeping you on your toes. He's exactly the type of man your parents warned you about.

Turning my attention back to my emails, I find myself wondering, is it really that terrible to date two men at once? Young, free and single, there's nothing to stop me from playing the field, but is it possible to play the field, without becoming a player?

Chapter 18

After locking up the studio on Tuesday afternoon, I make a quick trip to the little girl's room before heading to the car to wait for Lianna. As a result of breaking two nails at lunch, we arranged to go for manicures and a bite to eat in town. Watching the many people disperse from the revolving door, I fire up the engine as I spot Li heading my way.

'Sorry I'm late!' Pulling open the car door, she throws her handbag onto the back seat and climbs in.

'Do you have to treat your bag so badly?' I hiss, looking mournfully at the scuffed leather that was once so pretty. 'What has it ever done to you?'

'I am starving!' She exclaims, ignoring my handbag comment and checking out her perfect complexion in the mirror.

'When are you *not* starving?' I put the car into gear and pull out onto the open road.

She sticks her tongue out and fiddles with the radio. 'How have things been with the mysterious Mr Morgan? Are you excited about your dirty weekend away?'

'It's no big deal!' I say, trying to play it down before she blows it out of proportion. 'It is purely educational.'

'Educational. Is that what they're calling it these days?'

I turn the radio up in a bid to drown out any background Lianna noise, but she immediately turns it back down.

'When are you seeing George again?' She demands, turning in her seat to face me.

'Tomorrow...' I can't help but smile as Li screeches with excitement. 'We're going for coffee after work.'

Indicating to turn into the salon, I drum my fingers on the steering wheel.

'We should have pedicures, too.' Lianna muses, frowning at her chipped toenails.

'Good idea. I think I'll also get a wax...'

She raises her eyebrows and gasps. 'Oh, really? And I thought this trip was purely educational...'

*   *   *

Two sets of hot pink toes and a couple of French manicures later, we are sat in a pizza joint awaiting our food. Lianna has taken advantage of having a designated driver and is already knocking back a frosty glass of fizz. After her grilling earlier about George and Oliver, I decide to turn the tables on her.

'Is there anything you want to tell me?' I ask, remembering that Marc mentioned seeing her with a guy yesterday. 'Anything in the man department that might have slipped your mind?'

She pauses with her glass to her lips as a look of guilt washes over her face. 'No...'

I raise my eyebrows and rest my elbows on the table, knowing that it won't be long before she cracks.

'Okay, but please don't make a big deal out of it.' Taking a deep breath, she leans back in her seat. 'Dan and I have been talking again...'

I stare at her in disbelief, not quite knowing what to say. Lianna and Dan were an item for well over a year and to say she was smitten would be an understatement. They got as far as exchanging house keys before Dan got cold feet. It took Li months to get over him. I can't believe she would put herself through that again.

'I know what you're thinking, but he's changed!' She reaches out and squeezes my arm. 'Don't worry, it will be different this time.'

I offer her a tight smile and bite my lip. I know Lianna can handle herself, but I also know that Dan hurt her more than anyone else ever has.

'Just be careful. Don't fall too hard, too fast...'

Before I can give her a lecture, the waiter returns and places a basket of garlic bread on the table. Looking at my best friend, I can't help noticing she looks happier than I have seen her in a very long time. Her cheeks are rosy and her eyes are sparkling. It's just a shame that her joy lies in the hands of Dan.

When I was younger, I used to think dating would be easy. The reality is that dating is just a minefield and only the lucky ones make it to the end in one piece. My mind flits to my own love life and I wonder what my chances are of avoiding a broken bone, or worse, a broken heart...

Chapter 19

As I crawl around the office car park trying to find somewhere to park, I spot Oliver pulling his Audi into an impossibly small space. Waving my arms around trying to get his attention, I accidentally lean on the horn. Oblivious to the crazy octopus lady, he climbs out of the car and throws his bag over his shoulder.

Giving up, I swing my car into an adjacent parking space and peek at him in my rear-view mirror. He's with someone. A pretty, petite, blonde someone. A pretty, petite, blonde someone who goes by the name of Rebecca. I feel my blood run cold as I watch them laughing and joking as they head into the building. What is he doing with Rebecca? Why are they coming into work together? Did he spend the night with her?

Forcing myself to climb out of the car, I wait for a few moments to ensure we don't wind up in the lift together. Slowly walking across the foyer, I jump into the lift and ride in silence to the sixth floor. As the lift doors bounce open, I hesitantly step out and drag my feet towards the studio. Plastering a smile onto my face, I reach for the door handle and freeze when I hear Rebecca's muffled voice coming from inside.

In a desperate bid to hear what is going on, I press my ear up to the door and listen carefully. Their stifled voices are impossible to decode and I let out a frustrated sigh.

Striding into the studio I shoot Rebecca a strained smile as she floats past me.

'Everything okay?' Oliver asks, as I bang my handbag on the counter loudly.

Not replying, I tug off my coat and hang it on the back of my chair. Yes, I know I am being petulant, but I really can't shake how irked I am.

'Wow! You look fantastic!' He nods approvingly at my choice of outfit. 'Going somewhere nice?'

'Actually, I am.' I stare him in the intently and try to decipher his reaction. 'I have a date tonight.'

'Did we say tonight? I thought we said Friday?' He smiles back at me and flicks on his computer.

If he is bothered in the slightest, he doesn't show it. Feeling dejected, I hop onto a stool and flip through the pile of paperwork I have been putting off for days.

'So, who's the lucky guy? What's his name? What does he do?' Oliver asks, refusing to look directly at me.

My spirits rise as I realise I have got to him. 'His name is George, he's a barman.'

'A barman?' Oliver laughs and scratches his stubble. 'Way to shoot for the stars, Clara.'

'What's wrong with being a barman?' I retort, feeling a little protective over George. 'We can't all be high-flying designers.'

He shrugs his shoulders and returns to his computer.

'I saw you with Rebecca this morning...' I mumble, not being able to stop the words from escaping my mouth.

'I drove past her on the way here. It was raining, so I gave her a ride.' He says easily, stretching his arms above his head. 'Why do you care, anyway?'

'I don't care...' I bite my tongue and flip through the pile of papers.

Breathing a sigh of relief that nothing happened between them, I feel concerned by how much the thought of them together bothered me. Trying to ignore the growing tension in the room, I ask myself if the trip to Manchester is a good idea. The thought of being alone with Oliver makes the hairs on the back of my neck stand on end.

I feel like I am playing with fire and it's only a matter of time before I get burnt…

Chapter 20

I arrive at Dream Bean Coffee that evening and take a seat next to the window. Realising I'm early, I decide to decline a drink and wait for George to arrive. Thankfully I don't have to wait for long, as two minutes later, I spot him making his way down the street. Wrapped up in a huge scarf and bomber jacket, he looks completely adorable. I catch his eye and raise my hand, giggling as he fights against the wind to push his way inside.

'Hi!' I stand up to greet him and gladly accept a kiss on the cheek. 'How are you?'

'I'm good…' He peers behind me at the empty table and reaches for his wallet. 'Cappuccino?'

I nod happily as he heads over to the counter. Pointing to a huge slice of carrot cake, he holds up two fingers and passes the cashier his card. Carefully making his way back to our table, he shrugs off his jacket before passing me a hot mug.

As George fills me in on his lazy morning, I dive into the cake greedily. His lifestyle is so different to mine, our working lives are like night and day. I'm surprised to learn he has a History degree and disheartened when he goes on to say he has no intention of ever using it. Apparently, sleeping all day and chatting up partygoers all night is exactly what George wants to do for the rest of his days.

Oliver's words about him being only a barman ring loudly in my mind and I try to block them out. So what if he doesn't have much money, any responsibilities and a lack of career drive. George is a fun-fuelled free spirit and we could all learn a lot from him…

*   *   *

Saying my goodbyes to George, I feel a little sad to be leaving him so soon. I may not have fireworks when I'm with him, but he's so much fun to be around. His live and let live attitude fills the air the second he walks into a room. It's contagious and I'm a happier person just from being in his company for an hour.

I almost feel bad about going to Manchester with Oliver, but it *is* a work assignment. It's not like I'm dating Oliver. I'm not officially dating George either. For all I know, Oliver is just toying with me and to George, I may be just one of many.

Jumping into my car, I decide to call at Lianna's place on the way home and head towards her apartment. It's times like these when I regret not having a roommate, or something relatively lifelike to talk to when I get home. Maybe I'll get a budgie, or a life-sized cut out of Li to leave in the living room.

Cruising past the luxury apartment blocks, I pause to gawp at the prestige cars as I pull up outside her building. Large raindrops land on the windscreen and I brace myself for a soaking as I run across the car park. Jabbing at the intercom for what feels like an eternity, I'm about to give up when Lianna's voice drifts through the speakers.

'Hello?'

'Hi, it's me.'

'Clara?'

'Of course, Clara! Let me in, it's freezing out here!'

There's a rather a lengthy pause before she finally buzzes me through. Maybe the speaker is playing up again. Making my way to the fifth floor, I don't reach the second level before regretting my decision to take the stairs. No wonder Lianna is so thin. By the time I reach her apartment, I am panting for breath and red in the face.

Hearing muffled voices from inside, I rap on the knocker and perch on the windowsill to rest my wobbly legs. The door opens a few inches and Lianna pops her very ruffled head out.

'Hi! How are you? Is everything okay?' She babbles, frantically smoothing down her hair.

'Everything's fine. I just thought I would call in on my way home.' I look her up and down quizzically. 'Is this a bad time?'

'It's never a bad time!' She blushes and crinkles up her nose in embarrassment. 'It's just... *Dan's* here.'

I push open the door a little more to reveal a practically naked Dan on the couch.

'You're welcome to have a drink with us though...'

Dan waves and holds his bottle of beer in the air. 'We're about to order Indian food. Join us!'

I screw up my nose at the sight of his bare chest. 'You know what? I think I'll pass.'

'You sure?' Li asks, tugging up the straps on her camisole.

'Absolutely positive...'

Chapter 21

The next morning, I am dragging my case through the train station and trying not to fall over in my six-inch wedges. After my detour to Lianna's place last night, I spent the rest of the evening beautifying myself for my weekend away. I keep reminding myself that this is a work trip, but you can't turn up to a fashion exhibition with frizzy hair and a chipped manicure, can you?

Taking a seat on a rather hard bench, I glance at my watch and scan the platform in search of Oliver. The station is buzzing with people, each one rushing through the building in a hurry. I let out a yawn and try to pick him out in the crowd. Just as I am ready to give up, I spot a familiar face in the sea of people.

I stare for a moment, confused as to why he is so dressed up. He looks like a walking aftershave advert and judging by the many stares he is getting, I'm sure that every other female in the building would agree.

'Hey.' Oliver smiles lazily and props his suitcase up against mine. 'How's it going?'

'Good...' I take in his slick suit as he sits down on the bench. 'What's with the suit?'

'You like it?' He brushes some invisible dust off his shoulder and winks.

I smile back, feeling rather uneasy. I didn't realise this was going to be a super formal event.

'Don't look so worried!' Oliver squeezes my shoulder and I feel my cheeks flush. 'Relax!'

Pulling my travel case towards me, I fumble around in the zipped compartment. 'I have our tickets in here somewhere...'

'We won't be needing them.' He says confidently, running his fingers through his hair.

'Of course we will need them.' I let out a laugh and pull the tickets out of the envelope. 'I don't know how things work in America, but here in England, you need a ticket to get on a train.'

Shaking his head in response, Oliver reaches into his jacket pocket and produces two cards. My eyes widen as I squint at the small font and realise they're two First Class tickets to Manchester.

'But… but we already have tickets?' I stammer, looking at the cards in awe. 'Plus, there's no way that Marc would approve these on Suave.'

'Suave hasn't paid for them.' His eyes burn into mine as he steals a glance at his watch. 'I have…'

I stare at him, my heart beating faster than I ever knew possible. Just as I am about to question what the hell is going on, a smartly dressed stewardess appears in front of us.

'Mr Morgan?' She smiles sweetly and motions to the carriage on our left. 'Would you like me to escort you to your seats?'

My jaw falls open as I look up at Oliver. How does she know his name and why on earth would she be escorting him onto the train? Oliver happily accepts and stands to his feet, motioning for me to do the same. Totally lost for words, I grab my case and follow him on board.

Turning left instead of right gives me a rush of adrenaline. We walk to the end of the aisle and come to a stop at a luxury booth. The stewardess ushers us into our seats before disappearing behind a thick curtain.

'Why have you done this?' I gush, sliding into the booth and trying to hide my growing smile.

He shrugs his shoulders as a different stewardess approaches our table.

'Your champagne, Sir.'

I am on my third glass of champagne when the stewardess returns with a trolley of delicious food. Without saying a word, she begins piling our table with tiny cupcakes, finger sandwiches and a lovely new bottle of ice-cold bubbles. Thanking the stewardess, Oliver discreetly slips her a wad of notes.

'You still haven't told me why you've done all this?' I reach for my glass and wait for him to respond, my body warm and fuzzy from the alcohol.

'What can I say?' Oliver muses, pulling a small plate towards him. 'I like to travel in style.'

Deciding to drop it and just enjoy myself, I turn to look out of the window and sip my drink slowly. I watch the world whizz by in a series of complicated blurs until an announcement informs us we're just thirty minutes from our destination.

'I'm just going to run to the toilet.' Carefully sliding out of my seat, I hold on to the railing as the train wobbles beneath my feet.

'One more for the road?' Oliver asks, pointing to the remaining champagne.

'I better not. It's not even noon and we *are* meant to be working!' I shake my head and make my way along the carriage.

If you would have told me a month ago that I would be sitting in First Class, sipping champagne with a hot American, I would never have believed it. Slipping into the toilet cubicle, I feel a frisson of excitement as my reflection beams back at me. It just goes to show, you never know what is waiting for you around the corner...

* * *

A short while later, the train comes to a stop and once again a stewardess appears to escort us from the carriage. Grabbing our cases, we step onto the platform and make straight for the taxi rank. Manchester is a lot busier than I remember. The station is packed with people running in every direction, phones clutched to their ears, balancing coffee cups and stacks of folders. Joining the back of a taxi queue, I suddenly remember that I have no idea where we're going.

'Did you manage to change the hotel?' I ask, steadying myself on my suitcase. 'I still have the original accommodation booking in my case.'

'Maybe...' He shrugs his shoulders and I notice a smile playing on his lips as we step to the front of the queue.

'Where to?' The stocky driver asks, tossing our cases into the boot of the car.

Walking around to the driver's window, Oliver mumbles something that I don't quite catch and smiles mischievously. I fasten my seatbelt and stare out of the window at the busy street, watching the hundreds of people buzzing in and out of the shops. As we pull away from the kerb, I bite my lip as the driver puts his foot down. Why is it universally accepted that taxi drivers do not adhere to the Highway Code?

We whizz through the busy streets, turning left, right and left again until we come to a hard stop at a set of traffic lights. I glance over at Oliver, who is snapping away at pretty much everything, and let out a giggle. Catching me looking, he aims his camera in my direction.

'No!' I exclaim, covering my face with my hands. 'I hate having my picture taken!'

'Come on! Don't be such a baby!' He wrestles my hands away until we are interrupted by the driver, who slams his breaks on unnecessarily hard.

'The Valentina.' The driver yells, smiling in his rear-view mirror and pulling on the handbrake.

'*The Valentina?*' My heart skips a beat as I spin around to face Oliver.

Before he can answer, the taxi door swings open and a porter holds out his hand.

'Mr Morgan, welcome to The Valentina...'

Chapter 23

Taking in the ornate walls and antique furnishings, I feel my skin tingle with excitement. The delicate gold swirls in the plush burgundy carpet are brought to life by the twinkling chandeliers that hang overhead. I've heard amazing things about The Valentina, everybody has. I just never imagined it would be as incredible as this.

I watch in awe as Oliver hands our luggage over to the bell boy, who whisks them away in the blink of an eye.

'Champagne, Miss Andrews?' A beautiful young woman holds out a frosty flute and I happily accept it.

'Thank you very much!' I flash Oliver a smile and he motions for me to follow him.

We walk through the stunning lobby in silence, before coming to a stop at a beautiful gold lift. Glancing at my reflection in the glass, I can't quite believe that it is me staring back. Me, Clara Andrews, at

The Valentina! The lift doors glide open and we step inside, high on bubbles and adrenaline. The extremely professional porter stands in the corner, trying to be inconspicuous as we begin to shoot towards the sky.

The lift comes to a halt as the doors slowly sweep open and we walk out into the lobby. Taking in my surroundings, I realise there is only one door in front of us. Wait a minute? Why is there only one door? Where is my room? I am about to voice my concern when the porter opens the door and waves us both inside. It is not often that I am speechless, but I really am lost for words.

This is not a hotel room. This is the entire top floor of the building. Looking around in amazement, I try to take everything in. There must be at least five doors leading off from the huge living area. A velvet chaise longue is positioned in front of the giant windows, which provide an incredible view of the city. Walking around the corner, I discover a stunning kitchen, complete with an island and a million different gadgets. A colossal sofa is centred in the living space, adorned with velvet scatter cushions and a selection of intricate throws.

The porter slips out of the room, leaving Oliver and I alone.

'Well, what do you think?' He asks, striding over to the window and shaking off his suit jacket.

'I love it! It's beautiful!' I exclaim animatedly, twirling around in the open area. 'Where's my room?'

'Good question...' He walks around the couch and pushes open several doors before calling me over.

A squeal escapes my lips as I run into the room and jump straight onto the mammoth bed. 'This is amazing!' I cover my face with a cushion to hide my glowing cheeks, rolling around on the sheets like a child.

Oliver laughs and tosses a cushion at me. 'I'll leave you to get settled in.' He slips a room key onto the dresser and closes the door behind him.

Pushing myself up, I dig my phone out of my pocket and open the camera function. After snapping the bed, the view and everything in-between, I pick up a leather brochure from the dressing table. Shaking my head in disbelief, I run my fingers over the glossy pages. The Valentina offers more than you could ever dream of. It has two critically acclaimed restaurants, an award-winning spa, butler service and a world-famous cocktail bar.

Slamming the brochure shut, I pad around the room and slide open a heavy granite door to reveal a walk-in wardrobe. My three pairs of shoes and skinny jeans are going to look ridiculous in this enormous space. I imagine filling the wardrobe with designer clothing, prestige handbags and vintage accessories.

Lost in a world of silk and suede, my attention is drawn to a gold door knob at the far end of the closet. Puzzled, I push open the door and feel my heart race in my chest. The enormous bath, marble flooring and gigantic shower take my breath away. I run my hand over the bath and pick up the tiny toiletries one by one. Fighting the urge to strip off and climb straight in, I close the door and go back into the bedroom.

Leaning against the window, I watch the thousands of ant-like people buzzing around on the streets below and feel adrenaline rushing around my body. Why did Oliver bring me here? There is definitely more to this than just a business trip. First the champagne train journey and now this.

I flop down onto the bed and stretch out my legs on what feel like two million thread count sheets. Actually, I don't care what Oliver's intentions are. Right now, I really couldn't care less...

Chapter 24

Throwing a peplum dress onto the floor, I sit down on the bed and fold my arms in annoyance. I have to meet Oliver in the bar in ten minutes and I have *nothing* to wear. The lack of knowledge surrounding tonight's dinner is making the task of choosing an outfit even more difficult. How am I supposed to know what to wear when I don't even know where I'm going?

Realising that I'm going to be later than what is socially acceptable, I pull a black maxi dress off the hanger and tug it over my head. It's not perfect, but it's the best of a bad bunch. After adding a chunky bangle and a quick spray of perfume, I begrudgingly grab my room key and make my way down to the bar.

The soft jazz music is the first thing that hits me, followed by the sweet aroma of vanilla and spice. I glance around at the many beautiful people in search of Oliver. Heading over to the bar, I take a seat on a stool and order a cocktail. Watching the barman take a sparkling glass and expertly create the perfect concoction, I have another look around for Oliver.

Smiling at an adorable elderly couple, I almost don't spot him stepping out of the lift. Dressed in skinny jeans and a crisp white shirt, he spots me and raises his hand, causing my stomach to flip like crazy.

I smile back and quickly order him a drink. Considering he has paid for the room, I guess the least I can do is buy him a drink. Like lightening, another glass is placed down in front of me, along with a tiny paper slip. Picking up the receipt, my eyes widen in shock. This can't be my bill. I've only ordered two bloody drinks. Grabbing my credit card, I pass it to the barman with a queasy smile.

'Good evening.' Oliver props himself up on the stool next to me and I get a whiff of his familiar aftershave.

Pushing the glass towards him, I watch as he takes a sip and nods approvingly.

'Great choice...'

Giving myself a mental high five, I cross my legs to get comfortable. 'What did you do with your day?'

'I went to do a little shopping. I *was* planning on taking you with me, but I didn't wanna wake you.' Picking up his glass, he drapes his arm over the back of my chair.

Warmth washes over me as his hand brushes against my back.

'Well, I can always nip out tomorrow morning.' I mumble, trying not to be embarrassed that he obviously caught me napping.

He nods and fiddles with the stem of his glass. 'We should probably make a move. I've made dinner reservations.'

'Where are we eating?' I ask, immediately concerned about my state of dress, not to mention the strength of my credit card.

He jumps off his bar stool and holds out an arm to help me down. 'You'll see...'

Sipping the last of my dessert wine slowly, I lean back in my chair and revel in a fuzzy haze. 'So, Mr Morgan, do you treat all of your colleagues this well?'

'Only the pretty ones.' He stares at me intently, an unreadable expression on his face.

I look down at my lap as my cheeks flush violently. Once confident that my usual porcelain shade has returned, I work up the courage to ask the question I have been itching to ask all afternoon.

'What's all this about, Oliver?' My heart pounds as I fix my eyes on his, not really knowing what I want him to say.

'I like you.' He fires back, not missing a beat. 'Is that so bad?'

I feel my jaw sag, shocked at his forward reply. He likes me. He actually said it.

I'm still trying to find the words to respond when he speaks again, only this time, it's to the waiter.

'Can we get a bottle of champagne please?'

'Bollinger?'

'Bollinger would be great, thank you.'

I twirl my hair around my fingers and watch as the waiter expertly pops open the bottle of bubbles.

'Special occasion?' The waiter asks, as he pours the sparkling bubbles into two giant flutes.

'Yes.' I reply, locking eyes with Oliver.

How could it not be?

Chapter 25

I love it! Twirling around in the changing room, I watch the bright lights bouncing off the ruby satin. This has to be the most flattering dress I have ever worn. The square neckline flatters my ample cleavage and the skirt falls in large pleats, giving a slight retro vibe to the quirky gown. I turn around to see my favourite part, a delicate bow that sits neatly at the base of my spine. I *have* to have it. Without even checking the price tag, I drop it into my basket and drag my clothes back on.

When I opened my eyes this morning, I had an overwhelming urge to get out and explore the city. The sun was still rising as I crept out of the hotel room and wandered around the busy streets. I've really enjoyed spending a couple of hours alone. There's something rather magical about being at one with yourself in a strange place. Discovering things for the first time and taking in your surroundings is quite a magical thing.

Carefully placing the dress onto the counter, I take a glance at my watch and decide to head back to the room. The fashion exhibition starts in a few hours and I would like to make the most of the incredible en-suite.

'You've got yourself a bargain.' The sales assistant muses, carefully folding the dress. 'All occasion wear is half price this weekend. We actually have the shoes to match, if you're interested?'

I take in the low number on the till and I raise my eyebrows in shock.

At half price, it would be rude not to, wouldn't it?

* * *

Two hours later, it is just after midday and I am riding in the lift back to the room. Clutching my precious new outfit, I scan my room key and use my hip to push my way inside. The suite is deathly quiet as I dump my bags on the sofa and wander into the kitchen to grab a drink.

'Hey!' Hearing Oliver's delicious drawl makes the hairs on the back of my neck stand to attention.

I spin around to tell him about my successful shopping trip and drop my phone on the floor with a clatter. Standing in the doorway, wearing nothing more than a tiny towel, is a very wet, practically naked Oliver. Seemingly oblivious to my reaction, he strolls into the kitchen, leaving a trail of wet footprints behind him. Watching the beads of water roll down his back, I grab my phone and emit a high-pitched squawking sound before running to my room and slamming the door shut.

I perch on the edge of the bed and wait for my heart rate to subside. What is he trying to do? Does he *want* to give me a heart attack? Hearing his low laugh drift into the room, I feel my blood rush to my hot cheeks. He thinks he is so clever. He knows *exactly* what he is doing. Well, two can play at that game.

Stripping down to my birthday suit, I slip on my lace night dress and grab my favourite stilettoes. After fluffing up my hair and smudging my eyeliner, I stride back into the kitchen confidently. Out of the corner of my eye, I can see him stretched out on the sofa, still in the offending towel. Grabbing a bottle of water, I walk over to where he is sitting and take both of my shopping bags in silence.

Sashaying back to my room in what I hope is an alluring manner, I turn back to gauge his reaction.

'Uh, Clara?'

'Yes?' I reply seductively, draping myself against the door frame.

'You have underwear stuck to your shoe.'

Looking down in horror, I am mortified to see yesterday's knickers looped around my heel. Wanting the ground to swallow me up, I run back into my room and slam the door in embarrassment.

Damn, almost had it…

Chapter 26

'What about a movie?' Oliver asks, stretching his arms above his head and yawning.

'Do we have time for that?' Looking down at my wrist, I frown when I realise my watch is missing.

He nods in response and grabs the TV remote. Watching him flick through the channels, I jump up and grab a purple blanket from the back of the armchair. Glancing at the television, I'm appalled to see him scrolling through a list of horror movies.

'I hate horror movies.' Shaking my head, I pull the cover up to my chin and tuck in my feet. 'I'll be sleeping with the light on for a week if you make me watch one of those.'

Totally ignoring what I just said, he clicks *confirm* and switches off the lights with the control.

'Didn't you hear me?' I make a snatch for the remote, but he places it out of my reach and slips beneath the blanket.

Biting my lip, I sink into the couch and shake my head. He infuriates me, but one look at those big blue eyes and I turn into a giggling mess. How does he do it? How does he make me feel like a big ball of bashfulness?

As the film starts to play, I stretch my legs over the cushions and I notice Oliver's hand two inches from mine. My skin prickles as I watch him rub his thumb across the soft fabric. I know I should move my hand away, but I feel frozen. My arm refuses to move as he slowly edges closer, millimetre by millimetre, until his fingers are wrapped around mine. My heart pounds in my chest as he gently squeezes my hand, before pulling me over to him. Laying my head on his chest, I wrap my arms around his waist and feel my entire body buzz with excitement. This is definitely *not* in my job description.

*   *   *

Yawning loudly, I stretch out my arms and try to get my eyes to focus. It takes me a good thirty seconds to work out where I am and about another five to realise that Oliver's arm is wrapped tightly around my waist. Sitting bolt upright, I wiggle out of his grip and jump to my feet.

'Oliver! Wake-up!'

'What time is it?' He mumbles sleepily, pushing himself into a sitting position.

'I don't know. I can't find my watch.' I grab my phone and unlock the screen. 'It's almost seven! We've missed it!'

'Missed what?'

'The fashion exhibition!' I exclaim, throwing my arms in the air. 'The thing that we travelled over two hundred miles to go to!'

'Don't worry about it.' He stands up and puts his arm around my shoulders. 'Why are you so worked up?'

Instantly burning up at his touch, I bite my lip and look down at the floor. 'I went out before breakfast this morning to buy an outfit especially for it...'

Laughing, Oliver rubs his eyes and flicks off the TV.

'Well, why don't you throw it on and I'll take you out? We haven't travelled all this way for nothing.'

He lies back down on the sofa and kicks off the throw, along with his jogging bottoms. 'Go on then. What are you waiting for?'

* * *

'What do you think?' I spin around in my insanely cute dress and finish with a flourish.

'I think you look incredible.' Oliver winks and ushers me towards the door. 'Come on, let's go.'

Travelling down to the bar, I study our reflection in the lift mirror. We look like a happy couple on a romantic weekend away. No one would ever believe this was the result of an educational work trip. I feel his hand resting at the bottom of my back and move in a little closer, enjoying the tingle that is buzzing up and down my spine.

Walking into the bar, I take a seat at the nearest table whilst Oliver goes to get us some drinks. I am admiring a fellow guest's dress when a familiar cackle grabs my attention. Spinning around in my chair, I look around the room and try to pinpoint the ear-piercing sound.

No! It can't be! Blinking repeatedly, I grab my cocktail menu and cover my face. What the hell is *Gina* doing here? Peeking over the edge, I watch her stumble into the bar and prop herself up on a stool.

'Everything alright?' Oliver asks, giving me a rather strange look.

'Err…. yes.' I take the glass from him and put it down on the table. 'Thank you.'

Oliver pulls his chair closer to mine and drapes his arm over my shoulders. What is she doing here? Who is she here with? Unfortunately, I don't have to wait long to find out, as a moment later, Marc appears at the bar.

'Actually, no. Everything is not alright.' I try to whisper, but the hysteria wins, resulting in a high-pitched screech. 'Marc and Gina are here.'

'What?' His brow furrows into a frown as he looks around the bar. 'Who the hell is Gina?'

'Gina from work! She's with Marc over at the bar!'

Oliver follows my gaze to the bar and smiles as he spots them.

'Hey, Marc!' He waves one arm above his head until Marc turns around.

Understandably, Marc looks like he has just seen a ghost. After mumbling something in Gina's ear, he makes his way over to our table, hands stuffed firmly in his pockets. It wouldn't take a body language expert to work out that he isn't happy.

Feeling Oliver stroke my neck, I realise how bad this must look. Please don't sack me… please don't sack me… please don't sack me.

Chapter 27

'How's it going, buddy?' Oliver stands up and claps Marc on the back, oblivious to my impending panic attack.

Feeling the blood drain from my face, I stand up shakily and offer him an anxious smile.

'Hi, Marc. What... what are you doing up here?' Covering my mouth with my hand, I try to maintain a confident exterior.

'What am *I* doing here? What the hell are *you* doing here? I booked you into a hotel on Oxford Road.' Marc looks genuinely mystified. Mystified and very, very mad.

'I changed it...' Oliver laughs and signals to the barman for more drinks. 'No way I was staying there.'

Mortifyingly, Gina misreads this as an invite and starts to totter over in a ridiculous mini dress. Realising what is happening, Marc spins around at the distinct sound of clattering heels and tells her to stay put.

'I need to speak to you in private, Clara.' Shooting me daggers, Marc marches out to the lobby.

Not daring to do anything else, I roll my eyes at Oliver and run after him. I find Marc pacing up and down the lobby, looking extremely agitated. I take a moment to compose myself before taking a deep breath and walking over.

'Marc?'

'Clara, I really don't care what goes on with you two. As long as you don't bring domestics into the office, do what the hell you want.'

'Really? You're not mad?' Trying to play down my excitement, I twirl my clutch bag around my wrist. 'I thought I had to stay away from him?'

'Well, there isn't really much I can do about it.' He scratches his beard and folds his arms defensively. 'Look, I would really appreciate it if you didn't tell anyone I was up here tonight.'

I tilt my head to one side in confusion. 'Why wouldn't you want people to know that you were at the fashion exhibition?'

'The what?' Marc scowls, before a dawning realisation slowly creeps onto his face.

'Of course! The fashion exhibition! Yes, that's *exactly* why I am here.' He lets out a relieved laugh and pushes his glasses up the bridge of his nose.

'Why else would you be in a five-star hotel, two hundred miles from home with the delectable Gina Cockburn?' I wink playfully and give him a punch.

'Don't push it, Andrews.' As we start making our way back into the bar, Marc put his hand on my shoulder. 'And for future reference, it's pronounced *Co-burn*...'

* * *

After waving off Marc and a rather intoxicated Gina, I pick up my glass and turn my attention back to Oliver. He really is the most attractive man I've ever laid eyes on and from someone who's seen every Matthew McConaughey movie ever made, that's a big deal. Sliding my chair closer to his, I squeeze his arm before placing my hand on his knee. He looks down at me in surprise, before wrapping his arm around my shoulders. Now that I have Marc's blessing, kind of, I don't really have anything to lose and it feels pretty amazing.

'Refill?' Oliver asks, picking up the now empty bottle of champagne.

'Umm, I don't know. What time is the train tomorrow?' As much fun as I am having, I really don't fancy a two-hour train journey with a hangover.

'The train is whatever time you want it to be.' He looks at me carefully, his eyes glinting.

'In that case, yes, I will have a refill.'

Nodding, he reaches for his wallet and looks around for the waiter. 'You know… We do have a bottle of bubbles back in the room.'

I feel a fire burning in the pit of my stomach. We both know what he is really saying and I am pretty confident that it doesn't involve champagne.

'We can go back to the room…' Trying to act casual, I take my bag and push my chair under the table. 'I'm kind of tired anyway.'

'I seriously hope not.' Taking this a green light, Oliver grabs my hand and marches me to the lift.

The wait for the lift is agonising. We stand in silence, with Oliver running his fingers up and down my spine, tapping his foot in annoyance. Finally, the doors open and an elderly couple crawl out at a snail's pace. Flashing them a strained, yet polite smile, we dive in and jab the button repeatedly until the doors slam shut. Not daring to look at him, I stare down at my shoes and try desperately to ignore the growing tension in the air.

As soon as we arrive at our floor, I suddenly feel glued to the ground. With legs like lead, I follow Oliver to our room and wait as he unlocks the door. Fidgeting with my bag, I watch him walk into the kitchen and throw his jacket onto the couch. Skilfully popping a bottle of bubbles, he expertly pours out two glasses. Are we seriously going to drink fizz? Kicking off my shoes, I lean on the kitchen island as he pushes a glass towards me, not saying a word.

Locking eyes, I make my way around the kitchen until we are a just few feet apart. The smell of his aftershave makes me dizzy with anticipation. What happens now? I stare into his eyes, willing him to make the next move. As if reading my mind, he reaches down and tucks a stray curl behind my ear, before cupping my face with both hands. I can feel his breath on my cheek, causing every hair on the back of my neck to stand on end.

Closing my eyes, I wrap my arms around his waist and pull him in close. Staggering out of the kitchen we fall onto the couch in a heap. All the tension from the last few weeks rises to the surface like a firework. All the flirting, the lusting and the incredible tension that has been clouding the studio is coming to a head, right here, right now and it couldn't feel more right.

Chapter 28

Unhooking my legs from the mountain of bed sheets, I pick up a hotel dressing gown and slip out of the room. Grabbing a bottle of water from the mini bar, along with some posh crisps, I sit cross-legged in front of the huge windows. Opening the packet as quietly as possible, I watch the busy streets below. Lit up brightly by a powerful full moon, it looks just like a movie set. I wish I could freeze this moment. This glorious feeling of happiness and contentment is something I could bottle and wear forever.

Pressing my face against the cold glass, I glance over at the clock. 4:27am. Why on earth am I awake? You would think after all of tonight's excitement, I would be sleeping like a baby, but the adrenaline running through my veins Is acting like a double-espresso.

'Can't sleep?'

I look up to see Oliver leaning against the door frame. The room is in darkness, but I can see that he is smiling brightly.

'I'll be back in a minute. I was just a little thirsty.'

'Thirsty and hungry?' He gestures to the half-eaten bag of crisps and smiles. 'Fancy some room service?'

'Room service? It's the middle of the night!' I exclaim, as he takes a seat next to me and dives into the bag.

'So?' Reaching for the menu, he pulls me over so that my feet are across his lap. 'I'm ordering breakfast. Want some?'

I nod in response as Oliver kisses me on the forehead and pushes himself up to go and find the phone. Watching him place our order, my eyes land on his American flag tattoo and I am reminded that he will soon be returning home. Pushing the sickening thought to one side, I pull the dressing gown tightly around my waist and lean against the cool glass.

'All done.' He holds out a hand to help me up and leads me to the couch.

'England is way colder than I remember.' Shivering, he slips under the blanket and pulls me closer to him.

'What's the weather like back home this time of year?' I ask, resting my head on his chest.

'Oh, it's nice! Plenty of sunshine, maybe the odd shower.' He rubs my arm and entwines my fingers with his.

'So, when do you think you will be going back?'

'I haven't really thought about it. When my contract with Suave expires, I guess.'

Nodding sadly, I pull the throw up to my chin and scratch my nose.

'Hey, what is it?' Oliver gently turns my chin to face him.

'It's nothing, really...'

For a while, neither of us breathes a word. We just sit there holding each other in silence until Oliver speaks up.

'I really like you, Clara. So, I'm gonna lay my cards firmly on the table. I'm thirty-four, almost thirty-five. I'm done with the whole *dating* scene. I want kids, a wife and a family to call my own.' His brow furrows as he speaks, a genuine tone to his voice that I haven't heard before. 'Before I came over here, I ended a relationship because she didn't want to settle down. I know we haven't known each other for long, but I'm not up for playing games.'

I stare at him, dumbfounded. I must be dreaming. I have to be. Men don't want things like this! Men want one night stands and trips to Amsterdam with good-for-nothing friends. Pinching myself, I wince at the sting. Definitely not dreaming.

'Clara?' His voice snaps me out of my daydream and brings me back to reality. 'I'm just saying it how it is. I haven't got time for two-bit relationships. I want something real.'

I open my mouth to speak, but we are suddenly interrupted by a gentle knock at the door. We stare at each other for a moment longer, before Oliver gets up and pads across the room.

What just happened? What do I say? Do I want those things someday? *Yes!* Who wouldn't? Do I want them with a guy I have known for a matter of weeks? I really don't know. Wouldn't that be insane?

Trying to not explode with joy, I hug my knees and bite my lip.

I hear Oliver thanking the porter and watch him wheel in a trolley of silver cloches and yet another bottle of champagne.

'Champagne, seriously?' I can't help but laugh as he shrugs his shoulders and unloads the trolley onto the table.

The sun is starting to come up and the sky is streaked with beautiful shades of navy, orange and the odd slice of red. It's like it is being painted, one splash of colour at a time.

We both look out of the window, mesmerised as we watch the city spring to life. Light floods the streets, informing the entire population that it is time to get up. Dragging myself away, I take a seat at the table and help Oliver dish out the plates of fried treats. What would my life be like if this did work out? I stare at Oliver and wonder if it is possible to fall for someone you have only known for such a short space of time.

My mother used to tell me that true love takes time and patience to grow, but does true love always follow the rules?

Chapter 29

Throwing my cosmetic case into my suitcase I take one last look around the beautiful room. My humble abode suddenly feels a million light years away from The Valentina and I'm not overly excited about being reunited with it. Since Oliver's earlier romantic outburst, we haven't really spoken, but there hasn't been a moment that passes when I haven't thought about it. I know we are going to have to confront what he said sooner or later, but I haven't got a clue how to broach the subject and even when I do, what the hell do I say?

I have never met a man like Oliver before, a man so sure of what he wants and needs. It's so refreshing to be around a member of the male population that isn't afraid to address his feelings. I know Oliver isn't saying, *let's run away to a little white chapel and make a litter of babies right away*, but he is saying, *don't waste my time if that's not what you're not looking for.* The question is, what *am* I looking for?

After giving the penthouse a thorough check to make sure we haven't left anything, I rack my brains for what to say to Oliver. With him pouring his heart out to me, the least I can do is let him know how I feel. The thing is, I really do like him. I like him more than I have liked anyone for a very long time. Although I've been dating George, I feel a connection with Oliver that I don't want to let go. I keep reminding myself that I have only known him for a few short weeks and not to get carried away with lust and infatuation, but sometimes you just *know* when you have something special. Something that is worth holding on to.

'You ready, Clara?' I'm snapped back to reality by the sound of Oliver's voice.

Throwing his bag over his shoulder, he grabs my suitcase and holds open the door to the lobby.

'Yes. I am *definitely* ready.'

And I mean that in more ways than one…

*   *   *

The train journey back home is nowhere near as eventful as the trip up here, but sat next to Oliver, both reading books bought from the train station, I couldn't feel more at ease. In the past, I've always wanted to vomit at the sight of smugly happy couples, but being on the other side of the fence is really quite lovely. Enjoying my new-found status, I take a peek at my watch and finger the edge of my book. Just over forty minutes to go. Just over forty minutes to tell Oliver that I want the same things he wants.

We are at the far end of the First Class carriage with, only an elderly couple for company. Hearing them start to snore, I decide it's now or never.

'Oliver?'

Noticing my worried expression, he closes his book and raises an eyebrow cautiously.

'You know what you said to me last night, about wanting a proper relationship?' I feel my voice start to wobble and cough to cover it. How can I have a proper relationship when I can't even say the words without turning into a teenage girl?

Nodding in response, he puts the book into his holdall and suddenly looks rather serious.

I fidget with the sleeve of my jumper nervously. 'Could you not look at me when I say this?'

He laughs and turns to face the window. 'Sure...'

'I like you. I like you a lot. I just wanted to... put that on the table.' I hold my breath as I await his response.

'Tell me something I don't know.' He turns back to me and takes my hand in his. 'I'm not asking you to *marry* me, Clara. I'm just saying, I don't want to waste my time playing stupid school yard games.'

'Well, it's a good job we aren't in school then, isn't it?' I reach over and pull him in for a kiss, ignoring the disapproving comments from the now awake couple behind us.

*   *   *

The taxi driver opens the boot of the cab and drops in my heavy suitcase as if it's made of air. Fastening my seatbelt, I wipe the condensation from the window to reveal Oliver waving goodbye. I blow him a quick kiss and give my destination to the driver.

As the car speeds off down the street, I glance back at Oliver, who is climbing into a black cab. He looks up and waves again before slamming the door shut. Being back in London makes me question if this weekend ever happened. You know that feeling when you come back from holiday and the second your feet touch home soil, it's like you never left?

My phone bleeps and I wiggle it out of the pocket of my skinny jeans. Oh, no. It's George. I hesitate for a minute before opening the message.

Can't wait to see you on Friday.
xxx

My fingers hover above the keyboard, trying to find a suitable response. When we went for coffee last week, I agreed to go for dinner with him this Friday, but after the developments with Oliver, I really need to break things off with him. I know we weren't exactly *exclusive* or anything, but breaking things off via text message does seem a little callous. Deciding to tell him on Friday, I am about to put my phone away when another message flashes up on the screen. This one makes my stomach drop through the floor.

I hear rumours of a fashion exhibition in Paris next week if you don't already have plans...

Oh, mon Dieu.

Chapter 30

As I arrive at Suave on Monday morning, I am feeling rather anxious about seeing Oliver. I don't really know how I should act around him. Buzzing myself into the building, I take one look at the crowd of people waiting for the lift and decide to take the stairs for a change. Puffing my way up the many steps is more difficult than I anticipated. By the third floor, my thighs are burning and the soles of my feet feel like they have walked across broken glass.

I stop for breath when I finally reach my floor and cling to the handrail. I really need to get to a gym. My fitness level must be that of an overweight, diabetic pensioner. Once my breathing has returned to what is relatively normal, I head for the studio. I can see that the lights are on, which means Oliver is already here.

Peering through the glass, I watch him tapping away at his laptop, stopping to take the occasional bite of a massive bagel. Before he catches me peeping like a crazed stalker, I pull my bag over my shoulder and push open the doors.

'Good morning.' I flash him a nervous grin and shake off my coat. 'How are you?'

'Hey.' He immediately stands up and kisses me briefly on the lips. 'How are you?'

Taking a seat at the workbench, I try to work out how we are going to keep this professional during working hours. As if reading my mind, he flips through a sketch pad and places it between us.

'So, these Chelsea boots...'

Well, I guess that answers that question.

*　*　*

'So, how was Manchester?' Lianna passes me a slice of pizza and gets comfortable on the couch.

Nodding in response, I place my plate on the coffee table and clear my throat. 'I don't even know where to begin...'

Between bites, I start with the champagne train ride and continue right through to The Valentina. By the time I relive the amazing sex on the kitchen floor, Lianna is staring at me open-mouthed.

'Well, say something!' I laugh at her reaction and prod her in the ribs.

'Things like that don't happen in real life!' Pushing her glasses up her nose, she reaches for another slice.

'It doesn't stop there...' I stuff a few wedges into my mouth and wash them down with Pepsi. 'He told me that he wants a proper relationship. He actually sat me down and said he was looking for marriage, children, the whole thing.'

'It's like a Reese Witherspoon movie!' Her eyes are wide in shock as she pauses with a pizza slice to her mouth.

Feeling my face flush, I decide to turn the attention to her. 'Anyway, that's enough about me. What's going on with Dan? You know, apart from the obvious...'

'I'm not just sleeping with him, Clara.' Lianna's voice is suddenly serious. 'He's trying so hard to make this work...'

'What makes you so sure he's ready to settle down?' I look at my best friend, her eyes full of hope and expectation.

'I just know...' She's trying to sound confident, but her voice wobbles slightly.

'Have you seen anything of Marc lately?' I ask, deciding to change the subject.

'I haven't. He's been spending so much time with Gina.' She pulls a face and holds up her hands in disgust. 'I am starting to think that he actually *likes* her.'

Talk about there being something in the water. Lianna is settling down with Dan, I have been accosted by an ardent American and Marc... Well, I don't really know what Marc and Gina's situation is and I'm not too sure I want to find out...

Chapter 31

'This is *exactly* the vibe that we are looking for.' Marc scans the designs as he continues to ramble about the incredible quality of the leather.

It is just after four and we are sat in Marc's office submitting eight of our final designs. I still can't believe we have achieved so much already. We are way ahead of schedule and only need four more to complete the entire line. Feeling rather sad at the thought of my work placement with Oliver drawing to an end, I remind myself that he may become a permanent fixture in my life outside of the office.

'What about the snow boots?' Marc passes the folder back over to Oliver.

'Working on it, a couple more weeks and they will be finished.' He stands up and makes for the door.

'Excellent. And I have to say, I am very impressed.' Marc smiles and gives us a swift nod. 'Well done, both of you.'

Marc is so cute when he slips into professional mode. Straight-faced and affable, yet firm. You would never believe that he polishes off an ocean of Rioja and a chicken kebab every Saturday night. I shoot him a questioning look as he tries to silence his buzzing phone. The buzzing phone that hasn't stopped buzzing the entire meeting.

As we walk along the corridor, Oliver pulls me to one side by the fire exit.

'I was thinking, why don't you stay over at mine tonight?' His eyes glint under the bright spotlights as he lowers his voice to a whisper.

'I don't know...' I rest my hands on my hips and pout. 'I was planning on a night in the tub tonight.'

'We can still do that.'

'I was kidding!'

'Really?' He pulls me in close and nuzzles his face into my neck. 'I wasn't...'

Reaching for the pile of nachos, I drape my legs across Oliver's. Now I realise why he wasn't as taken with The Valentina as I was. This apartment makes the penthouse look distinctly average. I tip my head back and marvel at the amazing interior.

'I spoke to my folks this morning.' Oliver sighs and turns the television volume down. 'I told them I've met someone...'

Feeling my stomach drop to the floor, I bite my lip and smile nervously. 'What did they say?'

'They said, if we ever give them grandchildren, they have to be raised in America.' He looks at me seriously for a second too long, before breaking into laughter. 'I'm kidding! They're just happy I've finally found someone. Have *you* told anybody about us yet?'

'Just Lianna.' I hold my hair off my face before letting it fall around my shoulders. 'I didn't know whether you would feel comfortable with putting a label on it so soon.'

'I don't do labels, Clara.' He offers me a nacho and takes a slug of his beer. 'Not unless that label is husband and wife.'

My face springs into a smile as he pulls me towards him and wraps his arms around me. My head tells me it's far too soon to be committing to someone, but my heart is singing that this is right for me. Oliver is everything I've ever wanted in a man and almost unbelievably, he wants to be with me, too. I nuzzle my face into his chest and feel every muscle in my body relax. Right now, life is pretty much perfect.

Chapter 32

My first thought when I wake up on Wednesday morning is how amazing it is to be wrapped up Oliver's arms. My second, is to cancel with George for Friday and meet him tonight instead. I have to tell him that I can't date him anymore and I don't want to leave it a moment longer.

Rolling over, I prop myself up on my elbow and watch Oliver sleeping. His skin is toasty and warm as he breathes deeply, completely lost in a deep sleep. I resist the temptation to stroke his pretty face and instead let out a huge yawn. Reaching over for my phone, I manage to type out a quick text message before dropping it onto my face with a thud.

'Oww!'

A sleepy Oliver rouses at the sound of my voice and prises open an eye. 'Everything okay?'

'Everything's fine. I was just turning off my alarm.' Not wanting to admit that I was cancelling a date with another playmate, I slip the handset under my pillow and turn to face him. 'Time to get up, sleepyhead.'

'Just five more minutes.' He pulls the heavy duvet over our heads and wraps his arms around my waist.

'Mr Morgan, you are going to make me *very* late for work.'

'My bed, my rules.' He puts a finger to my mouth with mock severity. 'Now, roll over...'

* * *

Arriving at the office, I lose track of the many envious glances I accrue as we make our way to the studio. Of course, we are going to keep an air of professionalism during working hours, but it is clear to see that there is something going on between us, no matter how hard we try to disguise it.

Safely tucked away in the studio, I take off my coat and check my phone for notifications. No text messages, but I do have a missed call and a subsequent voicemail from George. Feeling rather nauseous, I shove my phone into my pocket and turn back towards the door.

'I'm just going to make a quick phone call…'

Oliver looks up from his laptop and nods, before returning to his emails. Tottering out into the lobby, I speed dial my voicemail. After listening to the obligatory pre-recorded message, George's cockney twang floods into my ear.

'Clara! It's great to hear from you! Unfortunately, I'm not going to be able to make it tonight. Hope you're still cool for Friday? Looking forward to seeing you. Let me know.'

Ending the call, I immediately feel incredibly guilty. I should call him right now and explain that I've met someone else. The problem is, how do I tell him without making myself sound like the village bike? I rack my brains for a good few minutes and get as far as a dialling tone before giving up. Deciding that the decent thing to do is to tell him in person on Friday, I take a deep breath and lock the screen. It's only two days. Forty-eight little hours. What difference does it make in the grand scheme of things?

I'm about to head back into the studio when I notice Marc's slick silver Mercedes pull up in the car park. Leaning on the window to get a better view, I let out a gasp as the passenger door opens and out jumps Gina. In her trademark tight dress and huge hoop earrings, she looks totally ridiculous and without being mean, a little plumper than usual. I stifle a giggle as they share a quick kiss, before strategically walking a metre apart into the building. Who are they kidding?

* * *

By the time I've dashed around the supermarket and dipped myself in a hot bath, I am dead on my feet. Crawling under my duvet brings such sweet relief. No matter how luxurious Oliver's bed is, no matter how soft his sheets are, nowhere quite feels like your own bed.

Kicking a leg out of the covers, I quickly pull it back in again when the cold air nips at my toes and it suddenly dawns on me how close to Christmas we are. I love Christmas, I always have. My mind flits to Oliver and I picture the two of us wearing matching snowman jumpers and silly paper hats.

I'm incredibly touched that he has told his family about us. Maybe I should introduce him to Lianna properly. I know she already knows who he is, but a double date with her and Dan sounds so much more appealing than taking him to meet my parents.

My eyes flit to the clock and I realise it's far too late to text her now. Making a mental note to arrange something tomorrow, I shut my eyes slowly and bury my face into the pillow. Before I know it, I am sucked into a magical dream world of gift wrap, fairy-lights and mulled wine.

Although I think for me, Santa has come
early this year. ..

Chapter 33

We are sat in the sandwich shop happily finishing off our lunches when Oliver springs the impromptu invitation on me.

'So, what do you say?' Looking at me hopefully, he waits for an answer. 'It's just a couple of drinks, that's all. No biggie.'

I look down at my boring black trousers and plain jumper dubiously. Hmm, more funeral than party. I envisaged myself dressed to kill when I met Oliver's friends for the first time. Remembering that I have a tiny can of hairspray and an old red lipstick in my handbag, I put down my sandwich. It's not much, but it's all I've got to work with.

'Okay...' I flash him a smile and reach for my coffee. 'I'll go.'

'That's my girl.' He gives my arm a squeeze and turns his attention back to his foot-long baguette.

As I sip my tepid coffee, I wonder what Oliver's friends will be like. He hasn't said much about his previous visit to England. Apart from him being quite young at the time, I don't really know anything else about it. Putting down my paper cup, I take a bite of my sandwich and feel my stomach flutter as he catches my eye and winks. It's not quite meeting the parents, but meeting the friends is a big deal and I intend to make it a fabulous impression...

* * *

Dragging a brush through my wild curls, I stare at my reflection in the mirror. In all honesty, I don't look *too* bad. The quick slick of red has managed to brighten my face up an iota and my hair still has some bounce from the last-minute blow-dry a few days ago. Satisfied that my appearance is acceptable, I make my way outside. Thankfully, Oliver is already waiting with a cab.

'Ready to rock?' He asks, holding open the door.

'Rock?' I exclaim. 'I thought you said it was just a few drinks?' Immediately panicking at the thought of being thrown into a nightclub with just red lips for confidence, my brow creases into a frown.

'Relax! It's an expression.' He ushers me into the back of the car and slides in beside me.

For the duration of the taxi ride, Oliver fills me in on the people that we are going to meet and I start to feel myself relax. Apparently, it's just some old friends he met whilst on his travels. We are going to have a couple of drinks and then go back to his place for dinner. In and out. Quick and easy. Telling myself to stop being so uptight, I rest my hand on Oliver's knee as the taxi comes to a halt.

After insisting on paying for the ride, I dive out onto the cold street and slip my hand under Oliver's arm. We are outside a series of luxury apartment blocks and I wait patiently as Oliver checks his phone for the address.

'It's this one.' He nods in the direction of the tallest building and pulls me along with him.

Pushing our way inside, I attempt to smooth down my hair as we wander along the lobby. Curly hair plus wind makes for one very dishevelled Clara. Stopping outside apartment thirteen, he jabs at the buzzer and smiles widely as the door swings open.

'Oh, my goodness! Hi! How are you?'

I try not to feel envious as a pretty blonde woman throws her arms around Oliver's neck and plants a pink kiss on his cheek.

'Lori!' He points to her tiny baby bump and laughs happily. 'Look at you!'

She laughs along and looks at me expectantly. 'And this is?'

Oliver puts his arm around my shoulders and ushers me towards her. 'This is Clara. My girlfriend.'

Almost bursting with pride, I hold out my hand for a shake, but she bats it away and hugs me tightly.

'So, *you're* the lucky girl who has managed to tie this one down? It's lovely to meet you, come on in.'

Her sickly-sweet voice is distinctly American and almost cartoon-like. She has cheekbones like razor blades and loose curls cascading down the back of a black wrap dress. We follow her into the apartment and I can't help being taken aback by the minimalist surroundings. Everything is white and glass, with the odd touch of pink dotted around.

One by one, people jump up as they notice who has arrived. For the next ten minutes, I am passed around the group, acquiring kisses, cuddles and the odd handshake. Once I am handed a cocktail and seated in a very comfy armchair, I finally start to enjoy myself. Lori and her extremely tall friend, Sarah, have been filling me in on Oliver's travels and all the mischief they used to get up to. I have laughed so much that my sides are beginning to throb.

'So, how long have you two been together?' Lori and Sarah are now huddled around my chair, questioning me about my relationship with Oliver. I glance over at him and smile as I hear his infectious laugh fill the room.

'Not too long, but things are going really well.' I feel myself blush and try to hide it with my cocktail glass.

'Well, you two are just *adorable* together.' Lori puts her hand under my chin and winks. 'We used to call him Peter Pan, the little boy who never wanted to grow up. It seems that time catches up with us all in the end.' She looks over at him and smiles fondly. 'It's nice seeing Oliver so happy.'

'Refill?' Sarah's husband holds out his hand for our glasses and I pass mine over.

Sarah jumps up and follows him into the kitchen, just as there's a knock at the door.

'Dammit! I really need to pee. Could you be a doll and just get that for me?' Lori holds her bump and races off through the sea of merry people.

Nodding in response, I fix my face into a smile before swinging open the door. Feeling momentarily paralysed with shock, my jaw hits the floor as I take in the man in front of me. What the hell is *he* doing here?

Chapter 34

George. I suddenly feel sick to my stomach. What do I say? What do I *do*?

'Clara?' George is staring at me with a look of astonishment and confusion on his face.

'G! You should have been here hours ago!' Lori is back and squealing with excitement. 'Where have you been?'

She pushes her way past me and wraps her lithe arms around George. Sensing my opportunity, I slink away into the apartment and scan the room for Oliver. My breaths are coming short and fast and I really think that I might pass out. Hearing George's voice get louder, I feel the blood drain from my already pale face. Frantically looking around for an escape route, I run over to the bathroom and slam the door shut with a bang. My fingers tremble as I fiddle with the lock and sit on the edge of the bath. I just need a plan. A plan. A plan. A plan. Think, Clara! *Think!*

'Clara? Hurry up in there! I've got more people for you to meet!' Lori knocks on the door repeatedly, until I finally give in and undo the latch.

'Are you okay?' She looks me up and down before bursting into hysterical laughter. 'Do you feel nauseous? Go easy on those cocktails! They kick like a mule.'

She has obviously mistaken my horror at George being here for me being a total lightweight. I manage a tight smile and begrudgingly allow her to pull me back into the minefield that is her living room. Thankfully, I can't see George, but I have noticed a herd of new faces huddled around the kitchen island.

'Guys, this is Clara.' Lori pushes me into the centre of the circle like a busker and I wave around helplessly.

'Hi, it's lovely to meet you all.' I force myself to smile at the dozen strange faces that are staring back at me.

'I think it's about time that we crack this bad boy open.' Sarah interrupts, waving around a bottle of champagne. 'Who's up for a glass of fizz?'

Glad to have the attention taken away from me, I join the others in a glass of bubbles and sidle over to Lori.

'Have you seen Oliver?' I ask, trying to keep my voice low.

'He went out back to see G's new car. Don't worry, he'll be back in a minute.' She smiles reassuringly, but I couldn't be more aghast.

'He's... he's with George?' My voice is suddenly so high, it makes Lori sound like a Barry White impersonator.

She nods and pulls out a couple of stools from the breakfast bar.

'G and Oliver go way back. Oliver used to say that he was a brother from another mother. You couldn't prise them apart. When Oliver went back home, they kind of drifted, but they still keep in touch. You know what men are like! They don't see each other for years, yet when they do, it's like they were never apart.'

I have been speechless before, but never thoughtless. It's as though my mind has been wiped and I have been left without any ability to form a sentence. Unaware of my shocked state, Lori carries on regardless.

'I'll introduce you as soon as they get back. They can't be out there much longer. They'll freeze to death!' She laughs loudly and beckons over Sarah.

I'm about to sneak out of the door when I spot George and Oliver coming back into the apartment. Without anywhere to hide, I sink into my seat as Oliver's voice becomes louder. This is it. This is how I am going to die. I feel a hand on my shoulder and immediately flinch at the touch.

'Clara, there's someone I want you to meet.' I glance up at Oliver, who is beaming down at me proudly and pointing at George. 'This is one of my old travelling buddies, G.'

Not daring to look directly at him, I open and close my mouth repeatedly as I try and find the correct words.

'Actually, Clara and I already know each other.' George takes a step towards me and I get a whiff of his familiar aftershave.

'Really?' Oliver looks down at me, understandably puzzled.

Not knowing what on earth to say for the best, I choose to say nothing and look down into my glass.

'Does someone want to elaborate on how you two know each other?' Oliver laughs nervously and slips his arm around my waist.

I steal a glance at George and notice him raise his eyebrows, visibly shocked.

'*Wow...*' George shakes his head and widens his eyes. 'You have got to be kidding me.'

'Does someone want to explain what's going on here?' Oliver's voice is now low and deep, with an edge to it that makes me nauseous.

'I'll tell you what's going on.' George bangs his hand down on the table and laughs sarcastically. 'You know the girl I just told you about outside? The girl that I had been seeing and thought it could lead to something special?'

Oliver just stares at him, gradually putting two and two together as the room suddenly falls silent.

'Come on, George. It was *two* dates!' I am trying to defend myself, but I know I'm just digging a deeper hole. 'I didn't know that you were friends...'

There are gasps from our audience and I suddenly feel like I am on the Jerry Springer show.

'What is going on in here?' Lori comes into the kitchen and eyes up the situation up anxiously.

'Clara's been cheating on Oliver with George!' Sarah shouts from the back of the room.

'I have not!' I shout, jumping to my feet. 'We went on two bloody dates!'

I turn to Oliver, but he backs away and walks out of the room, leaving me to face the already-decided jury.

How the hell am I going to get out of this one?

Chapter 35

I stare at the open doorway, not really knowing what to do. My head tells me to run after him, but my legs have turned to lead. My stomach churns as the magnitude of the situation hits me. I look around the room and take in the many angry faces. George has disappeared into the garden and is being consoled by a couple of Lori's friends. What the hell has just happened here?

'I think you should leave...' Lori holds out my handbag and points to the door.

Turning on my very high heels, I flounce out of the apartment and race down the hall. I get as far as the car park before realising that I don't have a clue where I am. Rummaging through my bag, I dial Oliver's number. It rings twice before being diverted to voicemail. Ending the call, I slip my phone into my coat pocket. Has he actually left me here? We can't leave things like this. The whole thing is ridiculous.

I haven't *technically* done anything wrong. Yes, I should have told George sooner that I couldn't see him anymore, but since things progressed with Oliver, I haven't had any intention of seeing George again. I was even doing the courteous thing by wanting to tell him in person. I knew I should have just sent a bloody text.

Looking around for clues as to my location, I wander down the street until I come to a fish and chip shop. Pushing open the door, I am immediately soothed by the delicious scent of battered cod and vinegar-soaked chips. Fish and chips make everything better, don't they? We will be curled up on the couch devouring these within the hour and all will be forgiven.

Quickly ordering some food, I hover in a corner to phone Oliver again.
Hearing his voicemail for the second time, my stomach starts to churn. I just need to speak to him and I can straighten all this out.

'Excuse me, your order is ready.' A very cute lady with a sharp black bob is holding out a plastic bag.

'Thank you...' I take the bag carefully and place it down beside me. 'I don't suppose you could phone me a taxi, could you?'

She lifts the receiver of a vintage phone and smiles genuinely. 'Where are you going?'

For a moment, I consider giving Oliver's details, but not being able to contact him isn't a sign that he's ready to talk yet. Deciding to give her my address instead, I type out a message to him.

I am so sorry, but this really is a BIG misunderstanding.
Just give me a chance to explain.
We will laugh about this in the morning.
Call me.
xxx

I hit *send* as a cab pulls up outside. Hugging the warm bag to my chest, I dash through the rain to the car. This is *not* how I pictured my night ending.

*　　*　　*

Dropping my fork onto the plate with a clatter, I check my phone for the millionth time. Still nothing. Since I arrived home, I have text Lianna, Marc and even my mother, but I haven't heard back from a single one of them. I am starting to think that my phone line is down. Telling myself that things will seem better in the morning, I take my plate and dump it in the dishwasher.

After a quick shower, I slip under the bed sheets and flick off the lights. My mind races as I stare up at the dark ceiling, replaying the events at Lori's over and over again. How has this gone so catastrophically wrong?

A tear slips down my cheek as my phone chirps from beneath my pillow. Opening the message, I feel my heart sink.

There isn't anything to explain.
George has told me everything.

You slept with my friend.
What is there to misunderstand about
that?

My sadness is quickly replaced with anger and I sit bolt upright. George said that I slept with him? I hold the screen close to my face and read the message again. I most definitely did *not* sleep with George! I slept at George's *house*. There's a world of difference. I turn on the light and dial Oliver's number, praying that he finally answers. Straight to voicemail, he's turned his phone off.

Not giving up so easily, I turn my attention to George and hold the handset to my ear. Quickly realising that it's going to ring out, I end the call and stare at the phone feeling completely defeated.

Giving up, I hold my head in my hands and try to formulate a plan to make everything okay again. Dating is supposed to be fun. It's supposed to be exciting and exhilarating. How has playing the field resulted in me being given a red card?

As I wonder where things went so terribly wrong, fury slowly seeps away and

I am left with an intense sadness in the pit of my stomach. In real life, it seems that no one falls in love and lives happily ever after and even those who do aren't guaranteed a fairy tale ending…

Chapter 36

I arrive at Suave half an hour early, armed with every breakfast option imaginable. After a terrible night's sleep, I awoke this morning with a fresh determination to make things right. There is absolutely no way I am letting this come between us. The whole thing has been blown completely out of proportion and is almost laughable.

Laying out enough food to feed a small army, I fold the napkins into paper swans and stand back to admire my handiwork. I am still marvelling at my delicate paper birds when I hear the studio doors squeak open.

'We need to talk…' Oliver drops his bag on the workbench and lets out a tired sigh.

Spinning around in my seat, I offer him a bright smile and pretend that I haven't heard him. 'I've brought breakfast! Bagels, baguettes, wraps and…' I trail off as I realise he looks completely dejected.

'I already ate…' Refusing to look directly at me, he pulls out his laptop and presses a few keys.

'Oh…' I know that he is lying, but I decide not to push it. 'Oliver, I need you to know that I did *not* sleep with George. Hand on my heart, I didn't. I went on a couple of dates with him before I started to date you. I even told you that I was dating someone, remember?' I look at him for his reaction, but he doesn't move a muscle. 'After Manchester, I decided I wasn't going to see him anymore. I was going to meet him tonight and break it off. I swear. You *have* to believe me.'

Finally bringing his eyes up to meet mine, I notice his face has turned red with fury. 'You were going to meet him *tonight*? After everything that we spoke about? My God, Clara! I told my parents about you! I introduced you to my friends!' He bangs his fist down on the table in anger. 'I feel like I don't know you at all.'

'I was meeting him to break things off!' I take a step towards him and he visibly recoils. How can he not get this?

'You know what, I don't wanna hear another word about it. We have three designs to finish this line, we don't have time for this crap.' Oliver sighs heavily and rubs his face. 'I just want to forget the entire thing…'

I run over happily and hold out my arms for a much-needed hug. 'I want to forget the entire thing ever happened, too.'

'No, Clara.' He backs away and puts his hands in the air. 'I want to forget about *us*.' Staring at me with glassy eyes, he shakes his head and turns away.

His words hit me like a bullet and I feel my bottom lip start to tremble. Not wanting to cry in front of him, I pack up the breakfast buffet in silence and slip out of the room. Heading for the stairs, his sharp words ring in my ears, making me feel physically sick. If only we wouldn't have gone to that party. I would have ended things with George tonight and everything would still be okay.

Arriving at the seventh floor, I paste a strained smile onto my face before making my way over to Lianna's desk.

'Hi...' I hand her the paper bag and manage a small laugh as the whiff of bacon immediately gains her attention.

'Hey!' She routes through the bag and widens her eyes at the mountain of food. 'What's all this in aid of?'

I shrug my shoulders and Lianna looks at me suspiciously.

'What's wrong?' Putting down her roll, she wipes her greasy fingers on a napkin.

'Nothing…' Hoping that she stops probing, I avoid eye contact and twirl a strand of hair around my finger. 'Are you free later?'

'I did have plans with Dan, but it's not important.' She smiles and returns to her sandwich. 'I'll come to yours after work.'

I nod gratefully and smile back. What would I do without Lianna? I watch as she unpacks the bag and proceeds to hand them out around the office. Coming back to her seat, she picks a piece of fluff off my jumper.

'So, is this a bottle of red and nachos kind of problem?'

Letting out a sigh, I blink back the tears that are pricking at the corners of my eyes. 'Actually, it's more of a bottle of vodka and ten pizzas kind of problem.'

'Okay...' She replies, her eyes widening with concern. 'Do you want me to bring Marc?'

I nod pathetically. I think it's safe to say I need as many friends as I can get right now…

Chapter 37

I have never been more relieved to get out of work. Today has been like a gerbil's funeral. Sad, strange and you don't *really* want to be there. After our heated exchange this morning, Oliver didn't say more than two words to me all day. I've never felt more alienated around another person in my entire life. I am so glad that Marc and Lianna are coming over shortly. I really need to vent my anger and get an outsider's opinion on the situation.

I stopped off at the supermarket on the way home and filled the boot with as much wine as possible, fully intending to drown my sorrows in a sea of Rioja. No sooner have I replenished the wine rack, there's a knock at the door. Peeping through the spy hole, I watch Marc and Li huddle under an umbrella. Both fighting for shelter from the rain, they push their way inside as soon as I open the door.

'It's freezing!' Marc grumbles, trying his best to balance three giant pizza boxes.

Whilst I lock the door, Lianna automatically marches into the kitchen and grabs a bottle of red and three glasses. Padding into the living room, I take a seat on the couch as Marc displays the pizza boxes on the coffee table. Once we are all armed with a glass of wine and a slice of pizza, Li plucks up the courage to ask what's wrong.

'What's going on, Andrews?' She tips her head to one side and purses her lips as she waits for me to respond.

I sigh heavily before taking a big gulp of wine. 'I'm glad that you have already got a drink in your hand, because you're going to need one after this...'

I recap The Valentina and our amazing train journey to Manchester, feeling awfully depressed as I recall the cherished memory. I watch Marc's jaw visibly drop as I tell him about the sex and the romantic declaration. Seeing their reaction to George being Oliver's old buddy almost makes me want to laugh and once I fill them in on this morning's heated escapades, they are both staring at me in deathly silence.

'Well…' I look between the two of them, waiting for their verdict. 'I haven't done anything wrong, right?'

There's an awkward tension in the air until Marc clears his throat.

'Not exactly...' He chooses his words very carefully, as though talking to a naughty child.

Holding my breath, I stare at him in shock and wait for him to elaborate.

'You *did* date two men at once. You were playing with fire.' Marc glances at Lianna, who is frowning at him furiously. 'How would *you* feel if Oliver had been dating someone else all this time?'

'I would be totally fine with it.' I lie, the thought of Oliver being with another woman making my stomach churn.

'You would not...' Marc retorts, shaking his head and taking a bite of pizza.

'I disagree.' Lianna coughs and jumps in on the conversation. 'Clara was a free agent. She went on a couple of dates with a couple of guys, big deal. When things got serious with one of them, she decided to do the right thing and break things off with the other one. It's just *very* unfortunate that they turned out to know each other.'

Marc rolls his eyes and reaches for more pizza.

'Anyway, I have known you to date *ten* women at once, so you can't say anything!' Lianna pushes Marc playfully and lets out a giggle.

'Not now, there's only one woman for me...'

I wait for him to laugh, but he seems deadly serious. Lianna shoots me a questioning look and puts her hand on his forehead. 'Are you feeling okay?'

'I've never felt better.' He dips a pizza crust in a dollop of mayo and reaches for his drink. 'Listen, there's something I've been meaning to tell you both...'

Lianna and I exchange concerned glances, both wondering what on earth is he going to say. Is he leaving Suave? Is he coming out of the closet?

'Gina's pregnant.'

I feel my jaw drop open in shock and automatically look at Li for her reaction.

Clasping her hands over her mouth, she looks like a startled blowfish.

'Just so we are on the same page, that's a *good* thing, right?' Li asks cautiously.

'It's an *amazing* thing! I couldn't be happier. We're both ecstatic.' Marc smiles and takes off his glasses to rub his eyes.

'Are you crying?' I exclaim, genuinely touched at finally seeing an emotional side to the usually sarcastic Marc.

'No! It's just this pizza, it has so many onions...' He rubs his face furiously and slips his glasses back on.

'Well, I think congratulations are in order!' I jump to my feet and grab a bottle of pink bubbles from the fridge.

'I've been saving this for a special occasion and I don't think it gets more special or more *surprising* than this.'

Filling three glasses with sparkling bubbles, I watch from the kitchen as Lianna throws herself at Marc. Seeing my two friends full of joy makes me temporarily forget about my own problems.

Marc having a baby with Gina has to be the most bizarre, yet weirdly adorable thing I have ever heard and I couldn't be happier for him if I tried...

Chapter 38

As the sun sets on Saturday evening, I still haven't heard anything from Oliver and my heart is physically aching. Giving my mobile a final glance, I dig my beautiful sandals out of their box and slip them onto my feet. When I was younger, I used to think a pretty pair of shoes fixed all of life's problems, if only that were true.

Over pizza yesterday evening, we decided that we would go out dancing tonight. Although Marc has used his *get out of jail free card* to nurse Gina through morning sickness, which she ironically gets in the evening, Lianna has managed to tear herself away Dan.

After the initial excitement of the Immaculate Conception died down, we returned to the subject of my messed-up love life. In the end, we all agreed that Oliver would come around eventually and if he didn't, it was his loss. The last part isn't something I am convinced of completely. Checking my phone for the trillionth time, I frown at the empty message folder and make for the door as a car horn beeps outside.

Making my way down the path, I try my hardest to avoid the muddy puddles and dive onto the back seat.

'Wow!' I gasp, running my hand over Lianna's dress. 'That dress is so pretty!'

As usual, Li looks stunning. Her Grecian-style dress is gathered down one side, falling perfectly around her knees.

'So, the plan is to have as many Cosmopolitans as it takes to put a smile on that miserable face of yours.' She pinches my nose and slips her arm through mine, before resting her head on my shoulder.

I manage a small smile before changing the subject. The single glass of red I had whilst getting ready is nowhere near enough to make me talk about Oliver. 'Can you believe Marc and Gina are having a baby? Hey, I wonder if they will get married?'

'I doubt it.' She scoffs, checking out her perfect manicure. 'I don't really see Gina as the marrying type.'

'Very true...' I agree, nodding along. 'But did you see Marc as the baby daddy type?'

She pauses for a moment, clearly thinking carefully. 'Good point.'

The cab comes to a steady stop and I pass a note to the driver before we head inside the restaurant. With the amount of alcohol I plan on consuming tonight, it's only wise to put down some solid foundations. And by solid foundations, I mean Indian food and lots of it.

* * *

'I swear, I had no intention of continuing to date George.' I wave my fork around wildly to emphasise my point. 'You do believe me, don't you?'

'Right, tonight is about making you forget about Mr America, not mope about him.' Llanna pushes my glass towards me and reaches for the mango sauce. 'Drink your cocktail.'

'I'm sorry. That's the last time I will mention him. I promise.' We clink glasses as our main courses arrive at the table.

Filling my plate with sugar, spice and all things nice, I listen as Lianna tells me all about the wonderful Dan.

'Well, I am very glad that you're happy, but enough of the soppy stuff! If I can't talk about how *bad* my love life is, I'm definitely not spending my night listening to how *great* yours is!'

'Fine...' She sticks her tongue out and picks up the drinks menu. 'Another drink?'

'Most definitely...'

Chapter 39

It's just after midnight and the club is filling up rapidly. All night I have watched the swarms of people buzzing through the door. One in, one out, like a conveyor belt of drunken ants. Music pulsates through my body as I prop myself at the bar and try to get the barman's attention. He immediately looks my way and I order another bottle. Passing him my card, I wait for him to swipe it, before weaving my way across the dancefloor.

'This is *definitely* the last one.' I slide into the booth next to Li and push my glass towards her.

The man who has spent the past hour trying to chat Lianna up has finally taken the hint and is now gyrating next to a mortified blonde woman. Watching her bat him away with her handbag, I take a sip of wine and tap my foot in time to the music. As dubious as I was about coming out tonight, Lianna has definitely succeeded in her plan to lift my spirits. I've secretly continued to check my phone every thirty minutes, but the disappointment in realising that Oliver hasn't called has eased massively.

Playing with the stem of my glass, I glance down at my watch as Lianna continues to ramble about her insane car insurance quote. I am still pretending to listen when I spot a tiny arm waving at me from the dancefloor. Trying to adjust my eyes to the smoke-filled room, I realise the skinny arm belongs to Rebecca. Before I can make an escape, she begins walking in our direction.

'Lianna?' I interrupt her mid-flow and she shoots me daggers. 'Rebecca's here...'

Lianna rolls her eyes and frowns with disdain. I have never understood Li's problem with Rebecca. Yes, she can be a little ditsy and a tad annoying, but she doesn't mean any harm.

'Hi!' Rebecca plants a red kiss on both of my cheeks and leans over the table to hug Lianna, who frostily pats her on the back.

Totally unaware of the icy reception, she plonks herself down between us.

'Have you had a good night?' I ask, sipping my drink and kicking a frowning Lianna under the table.

'We just got here!' Fluffing up her blonde hair, Rebecca whips out a mirror and checks her makeup.

'Who are you here with?' Lianna mumbles, peeling the label off the wine bottle.

'I'm actually on a blind date!' She squeals excitedly and looks over to the bar. 'He just went to get more drinks.'

'Don't you think you should give him a hand?' Lianna smiles at her sweetly, but I know this is just a way of getting rid of her. 'It looks pretty busy over there.'

'He *has* been over there a long time...' Rebecca slips under the table and straightens out her dress. 'Do you guys want anything?'

'We're both fine, thanks.' I gesture to the practically full wine bottle and flash her the thumbs-up sign.

'I'll be right back!' She runs her fingers through her hair and skips over to the bar.

Smiling in response, I bite my lip, not daring to look at Lianna.

'Do we *have* to sit with her?' Li folds her arms and leans back in her seat like a grumpy toddler.

'Don't be mean...' I rub her arm encouragingly, but she grabs her bag and jumps to her feet.

'I need to pee.' Swinging her bag over her shoulder, she storms off across the dancefloor.

Shaking my head, I look over to the bar for Rebecca and squint at the shadowy figures lining the counter. The music suddenly becomes louder and I dance happily in my seat, completely losing myself to the beat. I am still lost in my own world when Rebecca reappears at the table.

'G bought a round of tequila!' She squeals, placing a couple of tiny glasses on the table.

G? I feel my blood freeze as a tanned hand places a shot glass in front of me and I look up in disbelief. As our eyes meet, my stomach flips uncontrollably. An amused expression plays on his face as he stares

back at me, clearly enjoying this.
Snatching the tequila out of his hand, I throw back the golden liquid and wince at the burn. I've never needed a drink more...

Chapter 40

'G, this is my colleague, Clara Andrews.' Rebecca slips her arm through his and smiles up at him.

George looks down at me and I stare back at him in horror, neither one of us breathing a word.

'The queue was insane! Why does it take some women so long to pee?' Lianna grumbles, sliding into the booth beside me and immediately picking up a shot.

I glare at George, anger whooshing through me as his eyes burn into mine. Why on earth did he tell Oliver I slept with him? Why would he lie? What happened to that funny, kind man that I met only a few weeks ago?

'Where do I know his face from?' Li whispers in my ear, as Rebecca gushes about what a lovely guy George is.

'It's George!' I hiss, squeezing my hands into little fists. 'I have to talk to him...'

Clearly overhearing our conversation, George nods and follows me across the dancefloor. Slipping outside, I duck into a bakery doorway and wait for him to say something. Quickly realising he isn't going to speak up, I throw my arms in the air and let out a frustrated shriek.

'Why did you tell Oliver we slept together, George?' I take a step towards him and rest my hands on my hips. 'Why would you lie?'

Shaking his head, he stuffs his hands into his pockets and scowls. 'I did not tell Oliver that we slept together. I said you slept over. He just *assumed* that we slept together...'

'And you didn't think to correct him?' I interject, completely flummoxed by his reaction. 'I don't understand why you would let him think that?'

'*You're* the one in the wrong here, Clara. I don't think you are in any position to be pissed off...' George shakes his head and starts to walk away.

'I've not finished talking to you...' My voice trails off as I make a grab for his jacket and spin him around.

His brow is furrowed and I'm shocked to see he looks genuinely upset.

'I'm sorry, okay?' I stare directly at him, hoping that my apology comes across as sincere. 'I didn't mean to hurt either of you…'

George doesn't say a word, he simply pulls a packet of cigarettes out of his pocket and sits down on the kerb. Narrowly avoiding an empty pizza box, I take a seat next to him.

'I really didn't mean to hurt you, George. I tried to play the field and it backfired. It backfired massively.' I look down at the ground and wait for his response.

After a few minutes of prickly silence, it suddenly dawns on me just how wrong I have been. Why couldn't I see it before? Leading George into thinking we could be going somewhere whilst I was wrapped up in Oliver was an awful thing to do. Feeling incredibly guilty, I drop my head into my lap.

'I don't know what else to say, George. Just know that I am really, really sorry…' Giving up, I make my way back inside and squeeze through the packed club.

Catching Lianna's eye, I wave her over and pull my poncho over my head. 'I'm going to head home...'

Clearly sensing I am on the verge of tears, she nods and reaches across the booth for her coat.

As I wait for her to gather her belongings, I spot George ushering Rebecca towards the bar. Taking hold of Lianna's hand, I bury my face in my scarf and run to the door. Once we are safely outside, I feel my eyes fill with tears as we flag down a couple of taxis. Promising to call her tomorrow, I jump into the back and allow myself to cry. Once I start, I can't stop. I'm not even sure why I am crying. Losing Oliver? Knowing that I hurt George? I really don't know. What I do know is, I don't have a clue how to put it right...

Chapter 41

The following day, I am ashamed to admit that I only crawl out of bed to pee and answer the door to the delivery guy. By 8:30pm, I am huddled under my duvet, polishing off a tray of crispy seaweed. What a terrible waste of a Sunday.

I haven't been able to think about anything other than Oliver all day. I must have called him at least fifty times, but he didn't pick up and now I'm absolutely dreading going into work tomorrow. He still has three weeks left on his contract. How are we going to work together when he won't even acknowledge my existence?

Marc was right, you should never get involved with a colleague. Now, not only is my love life in tatters, my working environment is going to be near impossible to deal with. Feeling tears prick at the corners of my eyes, I furiously wipe my face and take a deep breath. Why do I never learn? Why can't I listen to people's advice and actually take it, instead of believing that I know best?

Burying my face into my pillow, I find myself regretting ever letting myself fall for Oliver. I knew right away it was a bad idea, I just couldn't stop myself. He brought to life parts of me I never knew existed.

My phone bleeps and I frantically scour the duvet for the handset. Seeing a scan picture flash up on the screen makes my heart sink. Marc is having a baby. He's creating a whole new life and I'm crying over a failed relationship. What has my life become?

* * *

'Clara?' Rebecca's voice rings in my ears and as my chest becomes excruciatingly tight. 'Clara, did you hear me?'

He's *gone?* What does that even mean?

'Clara?'

Finding my voice, I manage a squeak that resembles a *yes* and end the call. I repeat Rebecca's words over and over in my mind, desperately praying for them to be wrong. My heart feels broken as I stare at the phone in shock. Oliver has ended his contract and flown back to America. He's actually gone. I feel numb, I feel sick and more than anything else, I feel absolutely devastated.

A wave of nausea washes over me and I stick my head out of the window for air. The wind nips at my nose as the realisation of what has happened hits me. Running across the studio, I grab my phone and dial Oliver's number. It doesn't even offer one sympathy ring before diverting straight to voicemail. Hearing his voice makes my heart shatter into a million pieces. Is this it? Will I never see him again?

Refusing to accept this is over, I select Marc's number and tap my foot impatiently. He has to know more than Rebecca. He *has* to.

'Marc Stroker.'

'Marc? It's me. What the hell is going on?' Holding back my tears, I try to keep my voice steady.

'I'm sorry, Clara...'

Despite my best efforts, a sob escapes my lips.

'Oliver leaving like this has totally screwed us over...'

Marc's voice rings in my ears as I try to let his words sink in. This cannot be happening.

'Regardless of what was going on between the two of you, this line has to be finished. We have got just three weeks. There's no time to bring anyone else in. Do you think that you can manage on your own? If you can't, you just have to say the word.'

My entire body aches as my mind goes into overdrive. 'I'll do it...'

Marc continues to talk, but I stand frozen to the spot until the line goes dead. He's really gone. Even though I have been informed of this twice in the last five minutes, I still don't believe it. Not quite knowing what to do with myself, I take a seat at the workbench and bring up Oliver's designs on the laptop. Stroking the pretty sketches on the screen, I try to pull myself together. It took us forever to complete this design. We spent hours laughing, devouring doughnuts and reminiscing of cocktails at The Valentina as we put our ideas on paper.

Taking the fabric samples, I flip through the lace and printed canvases, telling myself that the show must go on...

*   *   *

If you don't count peeing or a trip to the water distiller, I haven't left the studio all day. Not even Lianna's offer of a trip to The Bistro could entice me out of the building. The little voice in the back of my mind warned me if I stopped working, I would crumble into a blubbering mess.

Locking up the studio, I head for the stairs and try to shake the feeling I have forgotten something. It's only when I jump into the car that I realise what is missing. Oliver.

Slamming the door, my heart aches as I contemplate how much has changed in just a couple of days. Right now, the future doesn't look quite so promising. Rain pounds against the window as I flick between the radio stations to find something that doesn't make me want to erupt into tears.

Giving up on the radio, I pull over and decide to give him one last try. Taking a few deep breaths, I dial Oliver's number and feel my heart sink at the strange ringtone. I let the line ring out for what seems like an eternity, before giving up and tossing my phone onto the passenger seat. I guess that's it. Resting my head on the steering wheel, I allow myself to sob as the phone starts to ring.

Not daring to look at the screen, I wipe my face and slowly put the handset to my ear.

'Clara?'

It's him.

'Clara? Are you there?' Oliver's husky voice comes down the line and my heart pangs with longing.

'Yes…' I squeak, so relieved to hear his voice again.

There's an awfully long silence, but just knowing that he is on the other end of the line is enough.

'You called?' He eventually manages, his voice flat and empty.

'I just wanted to hear your voice…' A tear slips down my cheek and I hear him sigh sadly.

'Look, I better go. I'm kind of in the middle of something here…'

'No, wait.' I sniff loudly and try to compose myself. 'I want you to know that I am really, truly sorry.' My voice starts to crack and I clasp my hand over my mouth to muffle the sobs.

There's another painful pause before Oliver clears his throat. 'I'm just sorry that it had to end like this. Goodbye, Clara.'

A click confirms the end of the call and I stare at the blank screen in shock. My skin stings at his sharp words as I let the tears roll down my cheeks. How can I be this upset about a man that has only been in my life for little more than a month? I've had haircuts that last longer. Having never had a real relationship before, I've never known what it is like to have my heart broken. I know now it's a pain that can't be paralleled.

Putting the car into gear, I debate driving over to Lianna's, but deep down there's only one place I want to go and that's home.

Chapter 42

Taking a giant mouthful of ice-cream, I hit *delete* and continue to scroll through the images. For the past half an hour, I have been wiping out every trace of Oliver from my phone. From our meal at La Fleur to The Valentina and silly selfies curled up on his couch, my photo album tells the story of our brief relationship in a series of snapshots. My shoulders become heavier with each photo I erase, until every last one has been permanently deleted.

Surely I am too old to be feeling like this over a man. I am not far from thirty and here I am, crying into a tub of ice-cream. Deciding I need something stronger, I abandon the dessert and go in search of the bottle of Jim Beam Marc gave me when I got promoted. Still unopened, with a thin layer of dust, it has been waiting around for a special occasion. Well, a special occasion or an emergency situation, one or the other.

Pouring out a rather larger measure, I let the strong fluid burn the back of my throat and warm me from the inside. Dropping onto the sofa and taking the bottle with me, I listen to the wind battering against the walls of the house. I have never been a big believer in the answer being at the bottom of a glass, but right now it's my only hope...

*   *   *

The following morning, I awake on the sofa with the glass still in my hand. My first hope when I open my eyes, is that the nauseating sadness has gone. Pushing myself up, I realise that it's still well and truly here, only now, I have a thudding headache to go with it.

Reluctantly heading for the bathroom, I turn on the shower and let the hot water droplets soothe my sore head. As the water pummels my aching shoulders, I decide that I've shed enough tears. I had a life before Oliver and I'm going to take that life back. It took me five years of dedication to get this promotion and I am not going to let all that work go to waste over a man.

Tugging on a pair of woolly tights, I dig around in my makeup bag for the brightest lipstick I can find. I might be broken inside, but my outward appearance is going to portray an image of confidence and togetherness if it kills me.

The many rom-coms I've watched over the years have taught me that keeping busy is key in getting over a breakup. Recalling this advice, I grab my phone and arrange lunch with Lianna. I also manage to make an appointment at the hairdressers and schedule a meeting with Marc to plan the final pieces for the line.

Satisfied that I am handling this rather well, I take a moment to scroll through my Twitter notifications and feel my heart tighten when my eyes land on Oliver's name. Before I can stop myself, my fingers tap on his photo. Staring at his picture, I feel all of my will power evaporate in an instant. Even on a four-inch screen, he still has the same effect on me.

The devil on my shoulder whispers in my ear that he's gone and he isn't coming back. Chucking my coffee down the sink, I tug on my coat and head for the door, telling myself you can't hold on to someone who has already let go of you...

Chapter 43

By the time that my stomach starts to grumble, my can-do attitude has worn paper-thin. Fiddling with my keys outside the office, I edge away from the smokers and check my watch. Lianna should have been here ten minutes ago. I am about to give up and head over to the pub on my own, when I spot her bustling through the revolving doors.

'Sorry I'm late.' Lianna pulls on her hat and digs the world's longest scarf out of her handbag. 'I was waiting on a call from HR.'

I give her a small nod in response as we head across the car park.

'How has it been with Oliver today?' She asks, linking her arm through mine.

My shoulders become heavy as I realise I have to tell her what's happened. 'He's gone…'

'Gone? What do you mean?' Coming to a stop at the crossing, she looks at me quizzically.

'He's gone.' I repeat sadly. 'He's flown back to America.'

'What the hell are you talking about. He's contracted to Suave. He can't have gone.' Lianna frowns in confusion as we walk along the busy street.

My heart hurts and I try my hardest to breathe through it. 'I don't know how and I don't know when, but he isn't working for Suave anymore and he's back in Texas.'

She makes numerous attempts at saying something, before grabbing my arm and dragging me inside the pub.

'When did you find out?' Li asks, taking a seat at a secluded table and shaking off her coat.

'Yesterday...' I mumble, not daring to look her in the eye in case tears start streaming down my face.

'Yesterday? Why is this the first I am hearing of it?' She leans across the table and places a hand on my arm.

'I didn't want to talk about It yesterday...'

'I think you *need* to talk about it.' Lianna interjects confidently. 'It's not good to keep negative emotions to yourself. Trust me, you will feel much better if you get it off your chest.'

The last thing I want to do is go over the whole thing again, but keeping it bottled up hasn't helped me one iota.

'Come on. Tell me everything...' She flashes me a reassuring smile and squeezes my hand.

And so I do. I start at the very beginning, with the unfortunate first meeting in The Bistro and my mortification when I realised he was our new designer. I smile fondly as I recall our first brunch together and the most romantic meal I have ever had in La Fleur. By the time that I get to the surprise champagne train ride and our sunrise heart to heart, tears are spilling down my cheeks once more.

He was perfect. Well, no one is perfect, but he was perfect for me. I loved him. I know it sounds insane to believe you could fall in love with someone so quickly, but I really, really did. Why haven't I realised it before now? It has been staring me in the face all this time.

'I love him...' Saying it out loud feels so right, it's like I should have been saying it all along.

'What?' Lianna's jaw drops open and she stares at me like I have finally gone insane. 'What the hell are you talking about?'

Shooting out of my chair, I chuck some notes onto the table and grab my handbag. Lianna makes an attempt to catch the money before it lands in her water with a splash.

'Clara!' She blushes furiously as people start to turn around in their seats at the commotion. 'Where are you going? Sit down!'

Running past the waiters and queuing customers, I push my way out onto the street. Hysterically emptying the contents of my handbag onto the pavement, I snatch my phone from the pile of hair slides and empty chewing gum wrappers. I am not having the only man I have ever loved walk away from me without a fight. Ignoring the comments from the angry pedestrians stepping over me, I dial Oliver's number. The line stays dead for a moment too long before clicking onto voicemail.

Desperately trying again, I hit *redial* and pray that he answers. Hearing the cold pre-recorded message, I feel a shattering devastation rising in my throat like bile. Before I can have a complete breakdown, a hand gently takes the phone from my grasp.

'Come on, let's get you home.'

I look up at Lianna and feel totally mortified by her sympathetic smile. Kneeling down on the pavement, she silently collects my things. The sight of my best friend coming to my rescue is the final straw. Allowing her to pull me to my feet, she bundles me into the back of a cab and gives the driver my address.

I don't stop crying the entire way home. I still have tears escaping my sore eyes when Lianna runs a hot bath and orders me to get in. It's only once I slip beneath the bubbles that I realise we haven't gone back to work. Too upset to care, I tilt my head back and let the water fill my ears, blocking out the rest of the world. My mum used to tell me that there isn't anything a long soak in the bath can't fix, but that was when my biggest problem was a bad case of period cramps. If problems are fixed by water, I'm going to need an entire ocean to sort this out...

Chapter 44

Pushing rice around my plate mournfully, I pretend not to hear Lianna and Marc whispering in the kitchen. Following my public meltdown earlier, I am feeling rather humiliated and I don't know what to say to move on from it. From what I can gather, they are both rather concerned about leaving me alone tonight.

'How are you feeling now?' Lianna asks, curling up next to me and stealing a chip from my plate.

'I'm alright and I'm so sorry about before.' My skin flushes crimson at the embarrassment of my friends seeing me like that. 'I don't know what came over me.'

'Don't be silly.' Lianna wraps her arm around my shoulders and pulls me towards her. 'Being upset isn't something to be ashamed of.' She looks over at Marc for encouragement.

'I never liked him anyway...' Marc winks at me over the top of his beer bottle and smiles.

'Let's watch a film.' Lianna suddenly declares, flicking through my impressive DVD collection.

Watching her study the titles, I pretend not to notice as she hides anything American or romantic under the coffee table.

As the two of them argue over which movie to watch, I slip out of the door and head for the bathroom. Leaning against the warm radiator, I pull back the curtain and watch the rain turn into murky puddles as it hits the ground. A loud bang makes me flinch and I look up to see the sky fill with green and red sparkles. Bonfire Night has always been one of my favourite celebrations, but even the impressive display can't bring me to raise a genuine a smile right now.

Letting the curtain fall back down I splash water onto my face before sloping back into the living room.

'Clara, come and get under here.' Lianna lifts the blanket up and shuffles over to make room.

Squeezing in-between the two of them, I pull the sheet up to my chin as the movie starts to play. I might be in a mess in the romance department, but I really do have some fantastic friends and with great friends by your side, you can get through just about anything...

* * *

It's gone midnight when I finally manage to convince Lianna and Marc to go home. The problem is, the second I close the door, I want to scream at them to come back. Fighting the urge to chase them down the street, I slowly walk into the living room and curl up in the armchair. Why do I suddenly feel so lonely? I have lived in this house on my own for four years and not once have I felt like this. Lianna spent all evening trying to convince me that it is normal to feel like this post-breakup, but I couldn't feel further from normal if I tried.

Deciding to call it a night, I flick off the living room light and pad into my bedroom. Pushing back the curtains to watch the fireworks, I open the wardrobe for some pyjamas. My hand lands on the red dress I bought in Manchester and my bottom lip starts to wobble. Memories of our trip come flooding back to me like a blow to the stomach as I close the door and crawl into bed.

As my tears soak into the pillow, I make a promise to myself that this is the last time I will cry over Oliver. Regardless of how much I want him, life is far too short and far too precious to waste it crying over things that you cannot change. Watching the sky light up with all the colours of the rainbow, I listen to the heavy rain rattling against the window.

Just as I am slipping into unconsciousness, a gentle knocking makes me stir. Pulling the duvet up over my head, I try to block out the noise. Quickly realising it isn't stopping anytime soon, I throw back the sheets and push open the window. The driving rain makes it extremely difficult to see as I try to get my eyes to focus.

I am about to retreat to bed when a black shadow catches my eye. Leaning out of the window, I can vaguely make out a silhouette of a man at my front door. Marc, no doubt. I promised him I would be fine, but I had a feeling he would be back.

Running down the stairs, I dry my damp face and fumble around in the hallway for the keys. The rain is making so much noise that I can barely hear myself think as I fiddle with the lock. Fighting against the wind, it takes all of my strength to pull the door open.

Squinting through the sheets of rain, I pinch myself to make sure I am not hallucinating.

'Oliver?' I whisper, taking a step forward and flicking on the light.

'Can I come in?' His eyes look tired, but his voice is steady and assured as he brushes his wet hair off his face.

I attempt to reply, but nothing comes out. Instead, I step aside as he pushes past me into the hallway, leaving a trail of soggy footprints in his wake.

'What... what are you doing here?' My knees tremble and I drop down onto the stairs for fear of collapsing.

'I love you.'

I hear the words tumble out of his mouth, but they take a moment to register. Stunned into silence, I stare at him in shock.

Crouching down to my level, he holds my shoulders and looks me straight in the eye. 'Clara, I have loved you since the day I first laid eyes on you. You had Pepto Bismol down your dress and vomit in your hair, but you were still the most beautiful thing I have ever seen.'

A laugh escapes my lips as my heart pounds harder and faster than I ever knew possible.

'I love you, too...'

And that's when he kissed me.

Wrapping my arms around him, I pull him in close and look up at the night sky. A giant firework explodes above us and for a split second, I truly believe that dreams really do come true...

Every once in a while, in the middle of an ordinary life, love gives us a fairy tale...

To be continued...

Follow Lacey London on Twitter

@thelaceylondon

Other books in the Clara Series:

The Clara series is exclusive to Amazon.

Also by Lacey London:

Anxiety Girl is exclusive to Amazon.

Meet Clara Andrews
Book 1

Meet Clara Andrews... Your new best friend!

With a love of cocktails and wine, a fantastic job in the fashion industry and the world's greatest best friends, Clara Andrews thought she had it all.

That is until a chance meeting introduces her to Oliver, a devastatingly handsome American designer. Trying to keep the focus on her work, Clara finds her heart stolen by Michelin starred restaurants and luxury hotels.

As things get flirty, Clara reminds herself that inter-office relationships are against the rules, so when a sudden recollection of a work's night out leads her to a cheeky, charming and downright gorgeous barman, she decides to see where it goes.

Clara soon finds out that dating two men isn't as easy as it seems...

Will she be able to play the field without getting played herself?

Join Clara as she finds herself landing in and out of trouble, re-affirming friendships, discovering truths and uncovering secrets.

Clara Meets the Parents

Book 2

Almost a year has passed since Clara found love in the arms of delectable American Oliver Morgan and things are starting to heat up.

The nights of tequila shots and bodycon dresses are now a distant memory, but a content Clara couldn't be happier about it.

It's not just Clara things have changed for. Marc is settling in to his new role as Baby Daddy and Lianna is lost in the arms of the hunky Dan once again.

When Oliver declares it time to meet the Texan in-laws, Clara is ecstatic and even more so when she discovers that the introduction will take place on the sandy beaches of Mexico!

Will Clara be able to win over Oliver's audacious mother?

What secrets will unfold when she finds an ally in the beautiful and captivating Erica?

Clara is going to need a little more than sun, sand and margaritas to get through this one...

Meet Clara Morgan

Book 3

When Clara, Lianna and Gina all find themselves engaged at the same time, it soon becomes clear that things are going to get a little crazy.

With Lianna and Gina busy planning their own impending nuptials, it's not long before Oliver enlists the help of Janie, his feisty Texan mother, to help Clara plan the wedding of her dreams.

However, it's not long before Clara realizes that Janie's vision of the perfect wedding day is more than a little different to her own.

Will Clara be able to cope with her shameless mother-in-law Janie?

What will happen when a groom gets cold feet?

And how will Clara handle a blast from the past who makes a reappearance in the most unexpected way possible?

Join Clara and the gang as three very different brides, plan three very different weddings.

With each one looking for the perfect fairy tale ending, who will get their happily ever after...

Clara at Christmas

Book 4

With snowflakes falling and fairy lights twinkling brightly, it can only mean one thing - Christmas will be very soon upon us.

With just twenty-five days to go until the big day, Clara finds herself dealing with more than just the usual festive stresses.

Plans to host the perfect Christmas Day for her American in-laws are ambushed by her BFF's clichéd meltdown at turning thirty.

With a best friend on the verge of a mid-life crisis, putting Christmas dinner on the table isn't the only thing Clara has got to worry about this year.

Taking on the role of Best Friend/Therapist,

Head Chef and Party Planner is much harder than Clara had anticipated.

With the clock ticking, can Clara pull things together - or will Christmas Day turn out to be the December disaster that she is so desperate to avoid?

Join Clara and the gang in this festive instalment and discover what life changing gifts are waiting for them under the tree this year...

Meet Baby Morgan

Book 5

It's fair to say that pregnancy hasn't been the joyous journey that Clara had anticipated. Extreme morning sickness, swollen ankles and crude cravings have plagued her for months and now that she has gone over her due date, she is desperate to get this baby out of her.

With a lovely new home in the leafy, affluent village of Spring Oak, Clara and Oliver are ready to start this new chapter in their lives. The cot has been bought, the nursery has been decorated and a name has been chosen. All that is missing, is the baby himself.

As Lianna is enjoying new found success with her interior design firm, Periwinkle, Clara turns to the women of the village for company. The once inseparable duo find themselves at different points in their lives and for the first time in their friendship, the cracks start to show.

Will motherhood turn out to be everything that Clara ever dreamed of?

Which naughty neighbour has a sizzling secret that she so desperately wants to keep hidden?

Laugh, smile and cry with Clara as she embarks on her journey to motherhood. A journey that has some unexpected bumps along the way. Bumps that she never expected...

Clara in the Caribbean

Book 6

Almost a year has passed since Clara returned to the big smoke and she couldn't be happier to be back in her city.

With the perfect husband, her best friends for neighbours and a beautiful baby boy, Clara feels like every aspect of her life has finally fallen into place.

It's not just Clara who things are going well for. The Strokers have made the move back from the land down under and Lianna is on cloud nine – literally.

Not only has she been jetting across the globe with her interior design firm, Periwinkle, she has also met the man of her dreams... again.

For the past twelve months Li has been having a long distance relationship with Vernon Clarke, a handsome man she met a year earlier on the beautiful island of Barbados.

After spending just seven short days together, Lianna decided that Vernon was the man for her and they have been Skype smooching ever since.

Due to Li's disastrous dating history, it's fair to say that Clara is more than a little dubious about Vernon being 'The One.' So, when her neighbours invite Clara to their villa in the Caribbean, she can't resist the chance of checking out the mysterious Vernon for herself.

Has Lianna finally found true love?

Will Vernon turn out to a knight in shining armour or just another fool in tin foil?

Grab a rum punch and join Clara and the gang as

they fly off to paradise in this sizzling summer
read!

Clara in America

Book 7

With Clara struggling to find the perfect present for her baby boy's second birthday, she is pleasantly surprised when her crazy mother-in-law, Janie, sends them tickets to Orlando.

After a horrendous flight, a mix-up at the airport and a let-down with the weather, Clara begins to question her decision to fly out to America.

Despite the initial setbacks, the excitement of Orlando gets a hold of them and the Morgans start to enjoy the fabulous Sunshine State.

Too busy having fun in the Florida sun, Clara tries to ignore the nagging feeling that something isn't quite right.

Does Janie's impromptu act of kindness have a hidden agenda?

Just as things start to look up, Janie drops a bombshell that none of them saw coming.

Can Clara stop Janie from making a huge mistake, or has Oliver's audacious mother finally gone too far?

Join Clara as she gets swept up in a world of fast food, sunshine and roller-coasters.

With Janie refusing to play by the rules, it looks like the Morgans are in for a bumpy ride...

Clara in the Middle

Book 8

It's been six months since Clara's crazy mother-in-law took up residence in the Morgan's spare bedroom and things are starting to get strained.

Between bringing booty calls back to the apartment and teaching Noah curse words, Janie's outrageous behaviour has become worse than ever.

When she agreed to this temporary arrangement, Clara knew it was only a matter of time before there were fireworks. But with Oliver seemingly oblivious to Janie's shocking actions, Clara feels like she has nowhere to turn.

Thankfully for Clara, she has a fluffy new puppy

and a job at her friend's lavish florist to take her mind off the problems at home.

Throwing herself into her work, Clara finds herself feeling extremely grateful for her great circle of friends, but when one of them puts her in an incredibly awkward situation she starts to feel more alone than ever.

Will Janie's risky behaviour finally push a wedge between Clara and Oliver?

How will Clara handle things when Eve asks her for the biggest favour you could ever ask?

With Clara feeling like she is stuck in the middle of so many sticky situations, will she be able to keep everybody happy?

Join Clara and the gang as they tackle more family dramas, laugh until they cry and test their friendships to the absolute limit.

Clara's Last Christmas

Book 9

The series has taken us on a journey through the minefields of dating, wedding day nerves, motherhood, Barbados, America and beyond, but it is now time to say goodbye.

Suave. It's where it all began for Clara and the gang and in a strange twist of fate, it's also where it all ends...

Just a few months ago, life seemed pretty rosy indeed. With Lianna back in London for good, Clara had been enjoying every second with her best friend.

From blinged-up baby shopping with Eve to wedding planning with a delirious Dawn, Clara and her friends were happier than ever.

Unfortunately, their happiness is short lived, as just weeks before Christmas, Oliver and Marc discover that their jobs are in jeopardy.

With Clara helping Eve to prepare for not one, but two new arrivals, news that Suave is going into administration rocks her to the core.

It may be December, but the prospect of being jobless at Christmas means that not everyone is feeling festive. Do they give up on Suave and move on, or can the gang work as one to rescue the company that brought them all together?

Can Clara and her friends save Suave in time for Christmas?

Join the gang for one final ride in this LAST EVER instalment in the series!

Anxiety Girl

Sadie Valentine is just like you and I, or so she was...

Set in the glitzy and glamorous Cheshire village of Alderley Edge, Anxiety Girl is a story surrounding the struggles of a beautiful young lady who thought she had it all.

Once a normal-ish woman, mental illness wasn't something that Sadie really thought about, but when the three evils, anxiety, panic and depression creep into her life, Sadie wonders if she will ever see the light again.

With her best friend, Aldo, by her side, can Sadie crawl out of the impossibly dark hole and takc back control of her life?

Once you have hit rock bottom, there's only one way to go...

Lacey London has spoken publicly about her own struggles with anxiety and hopes that Sadie will help other sufferers realise that there is light at the end of the tunnel.

The characters in this novel might be fictitious, but the feelings and emotions experienced are very real.

21123118R00162

Printed in Poland
by Amazon Fulfillment
Poland Sp. z o.o., Wrocław